heart of fury

BOOK TWO

VAMPIRE ROYALS OF NEW YORK

Heart of Fury
Vampire Royals of New York: Gabriel
Book Two
Copyright © 2021 by Sarah Piper
SarahPiperBooks.com

Cover design by Covers by Juan

ISBN-13: 978-1-948455-26-8

VAMPIRE ROYALS OF NEW YORK

Dorian

Dark Deception

Dark Seduction

Dark Obsession

Gabriel

Heart of Thorns

Heart of Fury

Heart of Flames

TAROT ACADEMY

Spells of Iron and Bone

Spells of Breath and Blade

Spells of Flame and Fury

Spells of Blood and Sorrow

Spells of Mist and Spirit

THE WITCH'S REBELS

Shadow Kissed

Darkness Bound

Demon Sworn

Blood Cursed

Death Untold

Rebel Reborn

THE WITCH'S MONSTERS

Blood and Midnight

CHAPTER ONE

The child stood behind the bar, no more than five years of age, still and gray as a stone. Blood had long ago soiled her dress, and her hair hung in limp locks to her waist, hopelessly matted.

She smelled of the old forests of home, damp and heavy with decay.

Gabriel hadn't seen her in nearly forty years—not since the night he'd marked ten years in Sin City. Ten years since his brother Dorian had nearly decapitated him and he'd walked out of Ravenswood without a backward glance.

That night, her dark eyes seemed to hold a particularly urgent warning, though he couldn't have said what it was. Any number of his choices deserved judgment. Scorn. His first decade out west had passed in a blur of gambling, booze, drugs, women, blood slaves—all part of the epic building of his empire and the search for that elusive *something* that'd left his eldest brother unrecognizable.

Obsession.

If Gabriel could find it, he'd reasoned back then—if he could lose himself so completely in the madness of some insatiable desire—perhaps he'd also find confirmation that he wasn't so cold and broken after all. That a heart could still beat passionately in a chest that'd long ago been excavated, even if it beat for something destructive.

But all Las Vegas had offered Gabriel was a constant ache for home, a fathomless hunger that made him dizzy on the best of days, and a mountain of sin he could never hope to scale—only to profit from. Immensely.

And, of course, there was the child.

He'd been alone in one of his clubs that night too, the last he'd seen her. And drunk. And no closer to un-fucking his life than he was now—more than two thousand miles, four decades, and hundreds of terrible decisions later.

Why the hell she'd chosen today to reappear, Gabriel knew not. Cared not.

"I can't help you," he told her, as he always did.

And she lingered, saying nothing, as *she* always did.

Never speaking. Never moving. Never aging. Merely watching him with haunted, empty eyes as bottomless as they'd been the morning she'd knelt beside her mother's corpse in the woods and shook the woman as if the force of her tiny fists had the power to awaken the dead.

Gabriel downed another shot of bourbon. Dragged the back of his hand across his mouth. "Take your revenge, girl, or leave me to plotting mine."

No response but the eyes, unblinking and ever watchful. Ever judging.

"I said leave me!" He whipped his glass in her direction. It passed right through her, taking out a bottle of rum on the shelf behind her in an explosion of amber and glass.

The girl flickered in his vision but didn't vanish, existing as she did in the space between all things. In his mind. In his memories. In the hell that surely awaited him on the day —sooner than he'd hoped, perhaps—a witch figured out how to end his immortal life.

"Bloody damned witches. Ghosts. *Demons.*" His lip curled back on the last word, thinking again of the woman who'd betrayed him. The monster he'd bound in the back of the club, still bleeding. "The whole lot of you can *burn.*"

Another shot, straight from the bottle this time, and a slice of mid-day sun spilled suddenly into the darkness, chasing off Gabriel's pitiful thoughts and the child both. He winced at the intrusion, the daylight a sharper pain than it was even a week ago.

The scents of his brothers flooded his awareness, irritating and impossible to miss.

"We're closed," he grumbled.

"For fuck's sake, Gabriel." Dorian approached with heavy, determined footsteps. Aiden followed behind, four newly appointed royal guards left outside. "Whose blood are you wearing now?"

Gabriel finally glanced up from his seat at the bar, where he'd been thoroughly floating his liver for at least an hour, and grimaced. Until Dorian had mentioned it, he hadn't even felt the cold, sticky wetness of the demon blood soaking his shirt.

"One who no longer needs it," Gabriel replied. "If you don't mind, I'd like to be alone."

"Actually, I do mind. I've been trying to reach you all morning." Dorian clamped a hand over Gabriel's shoulder, concern and exasperation warring in his gaze. "What the hell happened to you? Where's Jacinda?"

Jacinda. A tremor rippled through Gabriel's muscles. He hissed, forcing his attention to the bottle, lest he inadvertently choke his brother in the witch's absence. He scraped at the label with his thumbnail, watching the paper bits curl and peel away. "Don't ask."

"Lovers' quarrel?" Aiden took the adjacent barstool, looking over the smashed glass and spilled booze. Leaning close to Gabriel, he sniffed and said, "Doesn't smell like witch's blood."

"That's because it's *demon* blood, detective," Gabriel corrected. "A crucial difference all of us would be wise to learn."

Dorian narrowed his eyes. "*Which* demon? And if you tell me it's another of Chernikov's, we're—"

A sound like a wounded beast echoed from the deep recesses of the club, strangled and wet.

Gabriel rolled his eyes. Honestly, the fucking demon couldn't have been less compliant if he were Chernikov himself, resurrected from oblivion just to torment him.

Dorian's eyes widened. "And who the bloody hell is *that*?"

"The former owner of the blood. I've been questioning him."

"Questioning? Or torturing?"

"Potato, po-tah-to." Gabriel sighed. He almost wished the ghost-girl were back instead. A fuck lot easier dealing with *her* than explaining the events of the last twenty-four hours to his brothers—a thing he'd been dreading ever since he'd wiped out the mages at Shimmer.

Dorian turned toward the demon's choked sounds.

"That one's not talking," Gabriel said. "Trust me."

"He'll talk to *me*," Dorian said. "I've got a way with demons."

"And *I've* got his fucking tongue." He kicked the wet slab out from under the bar where it'd landed earlier, still slick with blood. Then, at Dorian's irate expression, "What? You told me I can't go round killing them. You never said anything about mutilation."

Dorian rubbed his forehead and sighed into his hand. "Still alive, then, I presume?"

"Caught in a devil's trap, going nowhere fast." Gabriel glanced toward the back of the club, the same shadowed booth where he'd recently taken out the demon Mikhail.

He Who Likes to Watch.

Gabriel hadn't bothered asking the new bastard's name —had no idea whether he liked to watch, too—but he'd plucked out his beady black eyes with a cocktail fork anyway. It was almost as satisfying as ripping out his tongue, though he didn't know where the eyes had ended up.

Perhaps Jacinda would happen upon them the next time she mixed one of her infamous drinks.

A bitter laugh caught in his throat, quickly dashed by his anger.

Dorian stalked back into the shadows, returning only seconds later, his face grim. To Aiden, he said, "Phone Isabelle, will you? We need to exorcise that monstrosity before he re-spawns and word reaches Rogozin."

"One more Chernikov castaway down. Pity." Gabriel let out a hum of mock sympathy, then took another swig from his bottle, the room growing fuzzy around the edges. Was it the booze? The curse? His own shite karma, finally come to bite him in the arse?

Dorian seethed. "I'll give you the benefit of the doubt and assume you had a good reason for this?"

"Thank you," Gabriel replied.

"The *reason*, Gabriel. Out with it." Impatience sliced through Dorian's every word, stabbing at Gabriel's gut, picking apart seams he'd been trying to stitch back together for their entire lives.

Beyond the burn of the liquor, guilt spilled into his chest, hot and prickly.

He hadn't wanted Dorian involved. The mess with Jacinda, the curse, Duchanes... Gabriel should've been able to handle it on his own. Between forging the new supernatural council, managing the ever-fraught Rogozin alliance, planning a fucking wedding... Dorian had enough on his plate.

Gabriel closed his eyes, the guilt simmering. No matter

how many centuries passed, he never stopped feeling like the errant little brother, running himself breathless to impress the others only to realize they hadn't even been watching him. "Dorian, I… I'm sorry. This wasn't—"

Sunlight sliced through the darkness again, silhouetting another vampire in the doorway and cutting Gabriel short.

"I was in surgery. I came as soon as I could." Colin rushed past the guards and into the club, bringing with him a blast of winter air. Shock filled his gaze as he took in the sight of Gabriel's blood-soaked shirt. "What happened? Are you hurt?"

"You called Colin too?" Gabriel asked.

"We were worried," Aiden said. "How much have you had to drink? It's barely noon."

Gabriel dropped his head into his hands and groaned. "For fifty years, this family existed in separate worlds without exchanging so much as a birthday greeting. Now I can't pass a single afternoon without fending off a barrage of needless concern? You're all bloody suffocating. I need more bourbon."

He slid off the barstool and headed behind the bar in search of another bottle. He found it, along with the scotch Dorian favored, and filled glasses for all of them.

"Tell me what happened, Gabriel," Dorian said with another sigh, the alcohol doing nothing for his dwindling patience.

"Well, let's see." Gabriel leaned against the shelves behind the bar and casually scratched his jaw as if he'd been asked for nothing more crucial than an accounting of his liquor collection. "Jacinda and I followed a promising lead on Duchanes last night, only to discover that the demon who provided the intel—" He thumbed toward the booth. "—was setting her up for an execution by a cult of mages calling themselves the Keepers of the Dark Flame. I slaughtered them, naturally, which had some *very* interesting side effects on my witch. I suppose that's because she's not a witch, but a demon. A hybrid, if we're being technical. I'm not sure exactly where the family tree branches off, but she also has a sister—an original succubus, of all things—who's now roaming the city, likely plotting its ruin. But take heart, brothers. The sister of the woman I so stupidly fell in love with happens to be the very demoness who bound Father's curse all those centuries ago. So..." He shrugged and downed his shot, then poured another, raising his glass in cheers. "One mystery solved."

"A *succubus*?" Colin said, at the same time Aiden said, "In *love* with her?"

"Yes," Gabriel said to both. "But the whole 'I'm plotting to rip out your heart later' bit put a damper on things this morning."

"Wait." Aiden blinked rapidly, clearly trying to find sense in a story that had none. "You're in love with a *succubus*? I thought you had it bad for the witch?"

"Keep up, Aiden," Gabriel said.

"Fascinating." Colin had the look—the same their father used to get when he'd made some new discovery. "I had no idea succubi could manifest outside the dreamspace."

Dorian took a bit longer than the others to find his words, and when he did, they exploded out of him in their usual dramatic fashion. "For fuck's sake, Gabriel! A mage cult? A succubus? The curse? What the fuck are you on about?"

"That's... too many questions in one breath." Gabriel slumped forward and laid his cheek on the cool surface of the bar, his eyes falling closed. The room spun, but he was beyond caring.

"Why didn't you call us sooner?"

Dorian again, his insistence like an ice pick to Gabriel's skull.

"Wasn't drunk enough."

"Clearly, neither are we." Dorian downed the scotch. Sighed. Refilled his glass. Sighed again. Then, in a voice burdened by the new weight these revelations would surely add to his life, "Start from the beginning, Gabriel. Leave nothing out."

Gabriel rolled himself back into a standing position and let the story spill forth—as much as he could remember through his bourbon-and-demon-blood haze. He told them about his search for Duchanes, the meeting at Shimmer out on Montauk, Jacinda's glamour magic, the mages.

The near-sacrifice that still had his stomach twisting into knots.

Thanks to some misplaced sense of loyalty—or, hell. Maybe it was shame at his own failure to recognize just how dangerous his little witch truly was—he didn't get too specific about Jacinda's response to the murders, saying only that the whole thing sent her into a kind of magical overdrive. He suspected they would've pressed him for more details had the next bit not commanded their full attention.

Viansa.

He told them about her break-ins—the one in his apartment as well as the one in his head—and everything Jacinda had deigned to share after the fact.

Far too long after the fact, as far as Gabriel was concerned, but there it was.

His chest tightened again with the hot, sharp sting of her betrayal. He washed it down with another drink, then said, "So it seems, brothers, the traitorous witch is not only half demon herself, but has somehow unleashed a dangerous succubus on this city—one who can't be smoked out. One who has the power of hellfire, the ability to get inside your head and turn you *right* fucking inside out, and a fierce determination to lay waste to any who dare oppose her."

Gabriel finally looked up at his brothers, finding every one of them staring at him open-mouthed, their faces paler than usual.

Dorian was the first to shake off the shock, quickly snapping back into authoritarian big-brother mode—Gabriel's least favorite.

"We need to find Viansa before she causes any more damage." Dorian pulled out his phone. "Did she leave anything behind?"

"We fought with her in my penthouse," Gabriel replied.

"There may be something she touched. That is—unless her sister's destroyed the evidence." He wouldn't put it past the witch. Demon. Whatever the bloody hell she was. "Who are you texting?"

"Cole. He should be able to pick up her scent from your apartment and track her from there. Hopefully, the trail hasn't gone completely cold." He finished firing off the text, then speared Gabriel with another scornful glance, his reproach slicing right to the bone. "Next time you decide to set the world on fire, brother, I'd appreciate the courtesy of a phone call."

"Cole can't help you," Gabriel said, trying to ignore the burn of shame in his chest. For fuck's sake, he'd been alive since before the invention of the printing press, yet Dorian had the uncanny ability to send him straight back to his childhood with a single raised eyebrow and a few curt words. "He's in Jersey, looking into those real estate leads on Duchanes."

"Bloody perfect." Dorian chucked his phone onto the bar, where it skidded right off and crashed to the floor.

"Hope you got the insurance on that one, mate," Aiden said, eyeing up the broken pieces. "It's D.O.A."

"Just like us if we don't clean up this mess," Dorian snapped. Then, to Gabriel, "What else can Jacinda tell us? Surely she can manage a locator spell. Get her down here."

"Jacinda can no longer be trusted—not that she ever could." Gabriel swallowed another shot, the alcohol burning as much as the admission he knew was coming next. "We need Isabelle."

"Never thought I'd hear such a thing from *you*, Gabriel Redthorne." The witch in question pushed through the doorway, limned in light and trailed by the faint scent of incense. She carried a leather case full of magical tools and potions—something she rarely left home without, now that she was bonded to the Redthornes and constantly on call, running interference on one supernatural emergency or another. "So what've you got for me, boys?"

Gabriel opened his mouth to speak, but Dorian took over instead.

"In no particular order," he said firmly, "an eyeless, tongueless Chernikov demon to banish. A deadly, mind-jacking succubus to track down. And finally, if it's not too much trouble…" He smacked the back of Gabriel's head in that special brotherly way that bordered on infuriating. "A drunken vampire to sober up, preferably before anything else goes to seed today."

"Hate to rain on your parade of endless optimism, Dori," Aiden said, "as pleasant as it always is. But…" He turned his phone to show them something on the screen—a video from a social media feed, the shot zoomed in on Union Square Park. The guy streaming it muttered something about "an uncanny experience" and "images that were definitely not safe for work." That was all Gabriel processed before the sight shocked him numb.

The whole area was packed with people—not unusual, given the holiday pop-up markets that lined the park pathways this time of year.

But rather than shopping for gifts, every last adult was

naked, engaged in the only activity that could possibly chase off the frigid December air.

"A spontaneous public orgy?" Isabelle grabbed the phone and stared down at the screen, her brow furrowed. "In broad daylight, in the middle of winter? And goodness, look at those poor kids!"

Children had been left to wander the park alone, some crying, some mute with confusion, all of them abandoned as readily as their parents' clothing, inhibitions, and minds.

Dorian closed his eyes and sighed. "It appears we've found our succubus."

CHAPTER TWO

"There! That's her." Gabriel pointed out a raven-haired woman in the crowd, naked and glittering like a jewel against the gray winter scene, her head thrown back in laughter. His skin crawled with revulsion at the sight.

But just as soon as he spotted her, she literally vanished. The naked revelers paid no mind to the disappearing act, but within seconds of her exit, the humans snapped out of their trance, scrambling in a rush of confusion and embarrassment for their clothing.

"Did you see that?" Gabriel asked. "Where the hell did she go?"

"If I had to make an educated guess," Colin said, scrolling through his own phone, "Columbus Circle." He showed them the screen—a different feed, streamed from a location more than forty blocks from the first.

Gabriel wanted to deny it—chalk it up to something in the air, in the water, just a bloody coincidence. But there she was again, black hair flapping like a dark flag in the wind, her nude body frolicking through the crowd as New Yorkers stripped off their winter coats in her wake.

"Is all of this live footage?" Dorian asked.

"Allegedly." Aiden flipped to another feed, finding the same Columbus Circle mayhem shot from another angle. Then, as if the passerby on the screen could hear him, "No, you daft bastard! No! Don't get any closer! And... There he goes. And that's.... *Wow*. Certainly not the brightest bulb, are you, mate? Humping a statue. What will your mother think?"

Behind the statue guy, Viansa laughed again, then vanished, leaving another group of very cold, very confused New Yorkers to quickly gather their clothes and dart away in mutual shame and fear.

"One of you had better fill me in," Isabelle said.

Gabriel did his best to relay the story, just as he had to his brothers. And all the while, Viansa continued to make the rounds, popping up randomly all over the city, grinning for every camera, dancing for every crowd, leaving them thirsty and breathless and ashamed.

"How is she bloody *doing* this?" Dorian asked, glancing at the latest feed—this one from one of the news networks that'd picked up the story. They were calling it an instance of mass localized hysteria, possibly related to a gas leak, urging people to stay home and stay calm.

Gabriel recalled the feel of the succubus rooting around in his mind—the insistent pressure, the loss of control.

"Hell hath no fury like a woman determined to take down the world."

"One stiffy at a time," Aiden added. Another incident had just broken out on the Upper East Side. "Bloody miracle, that kind of stamina. It's below freezing out there."

"My instinct is to go after her," Dorian said, "but I'm not sure it would do much good."

Isabelle shook her head. "We need magic. *Strong* magic. A binding spell, something to weaken or eliminate her power."

"Perhaps we could draw her to a different location," Dorian said. "Trap her."

The two of them tossed around some more ideas, but Gabriel was only half-listening. Now that the alcohol had faded, his thoughts were sharpening quickly.

This morning, after his fight with Jacinda, tracking down and torturing the demon had given him a purpose. A distraction. And later, when the feelings threatened to overtake him again, he'd drowned them in bourbon.

Now, they clawed their way back to his awareness, scraping and jabbing at his heart like rusty daggers.

Jacinda…

Even at a whisper, the name felt like a curse on his lips.

He couldn't stop seeing her face. Hearing her voice in his head. Feeling the silk of her skin on his fingertips, tasting her soft lips.

Devils *balls*, that kiss…

Don't stop. Just kiss me, Gabriel Redthorne…

He knew the promise she was making him, and in that moment, it'd felt like fucking *everything*.

Yet nothing about it was real. Just another part of her game. Her grand plan to ruin him and everyone else he cared about.

It was embedded in her hellspawn DNA. She'd admitted as much—she was created for the sole purpose of destroying vampires and ushering in the eternal rule of hell on Earth.

So why the fuck was Gabriel still fantasizing about that bloody kiss? He should've been fantasizing about her bloody head impaled on a pike, right next to her sister's. Two fewer demons in the world and a fuckload of a lot less misery.

"Gabriel," Dorian snapped, and Gabriel blinked away his thoughts, his brother coming back into sharp relief. "Answer the question."

"*What* question?" he snapped back. "I can't even hear myself think anymore."

Dorian opened his mouth, undoubtedly ready to unleash another lecture, but Isabelle placed a hand on his forearm, silencing him.

"The mages," Isabelle said evenly, her no-nonsense manner bringing calm to the endless storm of Redthorne bickering. "You said they were part of a cult dedicated to Viansa?"

Ignoring Dorian's death glare, Gabriel nodded. "Keepers of the Dark Flame. They had Jacinda on her knees, ready to slit her throat—that much I witnessed. This morning, she told me they'd planned to sacrifice her in a bid to bring back Viansa. I've no idea how that would've worked, but apparently, the succubus found another way."

"And these mages… How often do they meet?" she asked.

"The demon implied it was a weekly gathering, but that particular group won't be meeting again—not in this realm, anyway. I slaughtered them."

Images flashed through his mind—Jacinda on her knees. The sheen of the silver blade at her throat. The smell of fear and shit and blood.

So much fucking blood.

"But," Gabriel continued, forcing the gruesome memories aside, "they may have other factions. That was just one group—twelve mages meeting at an exclusive club out on the Island."

Isabelle nodded. "If they're involved with an original demon, then yes, it's likely there are more of them. A powerful being like Viansa wouldn't waste her time with a dozen men."

"And Duchanes," Gabriel said. "Evidence suggests they were working with him too, which means we can't rule out the possibility he's also connected to Viansa."

"Winning friends and influencing people as usual," Aiden said, rolling his eyes.

The group sat in silence for a few moments, marinating in all the possible ways things could go wrong.

Again.

"Do you have anything physical from last night?"

Isabelle finally asked. "The mage's athame? A garment containing their blood? I might be able to scry with it—see if it leads me to any clues about the group's identity or bigger mission."

"Nothing," Gabriel said. "After the slaughter, we ended up on the beach. The water... it washed us clean." Then, before she could ask any more questions about that particular scene, he added, "There was a Tarot card, though, now that I recall. Something with Scepters?"

Her eyes sparkled with new interest. "A Tarot card? You mean, in the ritual? Like part of a spell?"

"No, this was more like... like a calling card. Jacinda flashed it to the bartender before he revealed the meeting location, just as the demon told her to do."

Gabriel described it to her—the dark king with horns and a fiery scepter, riding a terrifying black stallion through a storm.

"*Lord* of Scepters?" Isabelle asked, alarm chasing the interest from her eyes.

When Gabriel nodded, she turned even paler than his ghost-girl.

"There are rumors of mages who've made dark bargains for direct access to hell's power," she explained. "They've adopted the Lord of Scepters as a sort of patron deity. These groups thrive on human sacrifices, forced demonic possessions, and myriad forms of ritual torture, all of it sanctioned by their leaders."

"No wonder they're so interested in the succubus," Gabriel said. "Sounds right up her depraved alley."

"I'm more concerned about Viansa's interest in them," Isabelle said. "What promises have they made her? What is she getting out of the arrangement now that she's manifested here, in the flesh?" She closed her eyes and let out a deep sigh, squaring her shoulders as if preparing for battle. When she glanced at him again, she said, "We need to get on top of this, and fast. I'm afraid the flagrant sexual mayhem is only the beginning."

"Now *there's* a name for a band," Aiden said cheerfully. "Flagrant Sexual Mayhem. I can already see the T-shirts."

Ignoring him, Dorian said to the witch, "Do you think these Keepers of the Dark Flame are connected to the group that wanted to flood the city with demons?"

Gabriel had the same thought. A couple of months earlier, Isabelle had alerted them to a demonic plot with ties to her father's business, Armitage Holdings—an illusion technology company Dorian recently acquired.

Led by Chernikov and Duchanes, a group of supernatural defectors had partnered with dark witches to bring more demons in through the hell portals. When that failed, they hatched a new scheme, hoping to fuse demon magic with stolen Armitage technology, leveraging the city's existing infrastructure to project mass illusions so terrifying and powerful, they'd bring the human population of New York to its knees, leaving them weak and desperate, easily swayed by a new demonic overlord.

Chernikov had since been assassinated, the larger plot foiled, but that didn't mean the threat was completely gone.

"I think anything's possible," Isabelle said, "and we

can't assume our battle with hell's residents is anywhere close to finished."

"We're in bed with some of those residents now," Gabriel said, struggling to keep the scorn from his voice. "Rogozin may be an ally on paper, but underneath all that glad-handing, he's still a demon. And now he's got some of Chernikov's former boot-lickers working for him."

"I'm aware," Dorian said firmly. "But Rogozin hasn't given any indication he's making a bigger play. He's aligned with us, which makes him one of the most powerful supernaturals in the city. Betraying us would mean striking out on his own and attempting to unite vampires and all the other supernaturals under his own demonic rule—not something they'd easily accept, especially if he gained his position through slaughter and subterfuge."

"Most of them have a hard enough time trusting *us*," Colin said. "And Dorian's trying to help them."

"Hence the need for the new council." Dorian poured himself another scotch. "The more we can involve the others, the more loyalty we can foster."

"In a perfect world, sure," Gabriel said. "Unfortunately, that's not where we live."

Lifting the glass to his lips, Dorian said, "I don't believe Rogozin would make a move this early into our partnership. We've only just begun putting together the council, sliding the pieces into place for a lasting peace. A hostile takeover would weaken his position. There is, however, another demon that concerns me in all of this." He lowered his eyes and sipped the scotch, the heavy silence gathering again, making Gabriel's skin prickle with unease.

"Azerius," Dorian finally whispered.

Azerius. A name they'd avoided speaking since the attack on Bloodbath, just like they'd avoided speaking their deceased brother Malcolm's name.

The two were inexorably linked.

When the Redthornes and their allies raided the club, Malcolm had shown up at the end, not long after the vampires had defeated their enemies and claimed Duchanes' property as their own. For weeks, he'd been betraying the family, working behind the scenes with enemy vampires eager to see the Redthorne rule over-turned. But on this day, Malcolm sealed his own fate: he tried to kill Charlotte.

The move left Dorian no choice but to attack. He stabbed Malcolm with the closest weapon at hand—the hell-forged Blade of Azerius. None of them had realized the sacrifice would summon the ancient demon lord himself, channeling his dark essence directly into Malcolm's body.

Dorian and Azerius fought a brutal battle on the rooftop. After what felt like an eternity, Dorian finally returned to them, covered in blood and ash, grief and anguish. One look into his tortured eyes and the rest of them knew. They just knew.

Against the odds, Dorian had defeated Azerius.

But Malcolm was gone too.

Like so much of their horrific history, their brother's inexplicable treachery and incomprehensible death was a festering wound that none of them would ever address—not directly, anyway. It would go where so many of the brutal, terrible things in their long lives had ended up, locked in the Redthorne vault of regret and loss, sealed away by silent mutual agreement, the slow passage of time, and copious amounts of alcohol.

Now, Gabriel, Colin, and Aiden seemed to be holding a collective breath, waiting for Dorian to continue, wondering just how deep he'd carve into that still-bleeding wound.

"After the fight on the roof," Dorian said, his tone measured, "Rogozin told me the demon lord hadn't actually died. The defeat merely banished him back to hell for a thousand years."

"Then what are you worried about?" Aiden asked. "You've still got, what? Nine hundred ninety-nine years and ten months, give or take."

"In theory," Dorian said. "But Viansa wasn't supposed to be able to manifest here either. We can't assume the banishment is foolproof. For all we know, Azerius and Viansa are intimately connected."

Aiden shrugged. "From the looks of these videos, she's got her hands full 'intimately connecting' with half the city right now. What good is a demon lord to her? He's in hell. If he weren't, I'd be writing your eulogy and divvying up your collection of expensive liquor by now."

Dorian nodded and drained the rest of his scotch, but Gabriel couldn't help but notice the tick of his jaw muscle, the tightening of his shoulders.

His eldest brother was worried.

"There are many powerful demon lords," Isabelle said. "And each one of them has dozens—maybe even hundreds of factions loyal to them. There's no indication Azerius is involved with Viansa or her larger plans to destroy the hell gates, but again, we can't rule it out. This is a long war, guys. An *immortal* war. It was waged long before you were turned into vampires and will continue long after House Redthorne passes into memory."

"So where does that leave us?" Dorian asked. "What's our play? We can't just let the succubus continue on unobstructed."

Turning back to Gabriel, Isabelle said, "If you could bring me something Viansa touched—or better yet, some part of her, like blood or a few strands of hair—I might be able to do a locator spell. But given the speed at which she's moving across the city, I don't know how helpful it will be. Our best bet is probably Jacinda."

Gabriel was already shaking his head. "I told you. The witch can't be trusted."

"Viansa is her *sister*, Gabriel. We can't dismiss Jacinda's insights just because she withheld information from you."

"Withheld information?" He nearly laughed. "Isabelle, this isn't some schoolyard game of secrets. She knew the dangers her sister posed—knew the succubus was responsible for binding our curse. She deliberately misled me at every turn, put all of our lives at risk, put this entire *city* at risk, and let's not forget—Jacinda herself is part demon. A bloody hybrid created to destroy us all. The woman makes the Rogozin partnership look like a match made in heaven."

"Maybe so," Isabelle said. "But that hybrid is also our best chance at finding Viansa and preventing the entire city from collapsing into a sex-induced coma. And something tells me that's not even her endgame."

"Just the foreplay," Aiden said, cracking up at his own joke.

Dorian scoffed. "Remind me next time to leave you home."

"And miss the chance to see you and the princelings go down in a blaze of glory over yet *another* supernatural crisis? No way. I paid good money for these front-row seats."

Immune to Aiden's nonsense, Isabelle cupped Gabriel's cheek, her touch as comforting as a mother's. In a soft voice, she said, "What would you like me to do then, Gabriel? I can't help you if you won't let me."

Gabriel closed his eyes and exhaled, slow and deep.

That was the fucking question, wasn't it? What *would* he like her to do?

What the fuck was *he* supposed to do? With his brothers? With this new threat? With the witch he still—despite everything she'd put him through—couldn't get out of his fucking head? Couldn't get out of the very heart she'd planned to destroy?

He opened his eyes and shook off Isabelle's touch—a kindness he didn't deserve. "I would like you to deal with the demon exorcism. I'll deal with Jacinda and meet you back here in an hour."

"How, precisely, are you planning to deal with her?" she asked.

Gabriel glanced at the booth where the demon bastard still sat, moaning incoherently, stinking up the place. He looked at Dorian, recalling Azerius, recalling Malcolm, recalling their father, recalling all the things that had threatened to destroy their family over the centuries—all the things they'd somehow, despite the odds, survived.

So far.

Gabriel donned his sunglasses and headed for the exit, his response a faint whisper that lingered in his wake.

"I will deal with her in the same manner *all* traitors must be dealt with."

CHAPTER THREE

Blood dripped down the bathroom mirror, sliding into the marble sink in deep, ruby-red swirls. It reminded Jaci of the peppermint candies all the shops and restaurants kept in little bowls by the cash registers during the holidays.

But there was nothing festive about a demon summoning. Especially when the demon she so desperately needed to reach wasn't picking up.

"Come on, Meech," she said, pacing the bathroom. Flickering candlelight threw harsh shadows on the wall, casting the room in an eerie glow. "Be there. Fucking *be* there."

No response. Again.

After hours of failed attempts, Jaci was damn near crawling out of her skin with worry.

She stopped pacing and glanced again at the mirror.

Not even a glimmer of hellfire shone from the other side.

It should've worked. It wasn't like before when she'd had to improvise with the apples and broken glass during her first few days at the apartment. Now, Jaci had her proper summoning potions, her anointed black candles, the athame—all the magical tools that'd made connecting with her cousin possible in the past.

But even with all the right tools and Jaci's ceaseless efforts, Meech refused to appear.

Gripping the edge of the sink, she leaned forward, nose-to-nose with her own blood-streaked reflection. Her eyes were red and glassy, her hair a wild tangle. She hadn't even changed out of the damned dress from last night. It was singed with hellfire from her fight with Viansa, stinking of brimstone.

Stinking of her childhood.

Jaci swallowed back a wave of nausea. She'd never looked so unhinged. So broken.

"Meech, I swear to the devil if you don't answer me, I'll march straight into hell and kill you myself."

Jaci continued to glare.

Her reflection glared back.

Meech, unfortunately, did not.

Panic crawled through her chest, but succumbing to it would only lead to more mistakes. And right now, she couldn't afford a single fuck-up.

On the back edge of the sink, a Tarot card leaned against a large pillar candle, its top border dark with melted black wax.

The Queen of Knives.

She lifted the card and gazed into the image—a silver-haired queen seated on her throne, a black dagger clutched in both hands. One gripped the handle, the other the blade, her pale skin and white dress splattered with blood. Just over her shoulder, a raven perched, watching.

The Queen was known for swiftness and clarity, an uncanny ability to cut through bullshit, and a spine of steel. One look into those silver-blue eyes, and Jaci could practically hear the challenge in her voice. The warning.

Fucking try me, she seemed to say.

Jaci wanted that Queen on her side. Wanted her to help her cut through whatever dark, murky veil had clouded her connection to Meech.

"Help me," she begged, calling on the Queen's magic.

The Queen returned her deep gaze, silent but for the new energy suddenly buzzing across Jaci's skin. She pressed the card to her chest and placed her other palm flat against the mirror, closing her eyes and filling her mind with thoughts of her cousin.

Her sly smile, her contagious laughter, the outrageous purple hair.

The magic crested, filling and warming her from the inside out. Just before it peaked, she opened her eyes and stared into the mirror once more, reaching out with her mind. Her heart. Her soul. Everything she had, all of it amplified by the magic coursing through her.

"Demetria," she whispered.

The magic flared hot, making her skin glow.

Her reflection wavered, and hope surged in Jaci's heart.

But after another few beats, all that appeared in the mirror were the toxic, yellow-green flames of one of hell's most vicious realms.

She'd tapped into the place, but not the demon. Not the cousin who was more like a sister than her own flesh and blood had ever been.

Jaci dropped the Tarot card, the Queen of Knives landing in the blood-swirled sink as if the card itself had come to life, spilling her own blood only to watch it trickle down the drain into nothing.

One by one, she blew out the candles. Cleaned off the mirror. Plucked the card out of the sink and washed away the rest of the blood until once more, the bathroom was back to neutral.

Washing her hands, Jaci tried to reason out the possibilities.

Best-case scenario? Meech was off in one of the other realms dealing with whatever hell business kept her busy these days. Maybe Viansa had stirred up a bunch of shit down there before finally manifesting here, and now Meech was scrambling to clean up the mess.

It was also possible Viansa *had* gotten to Meech—but hadn't killed her. Maybe the bitch was holding her captive, waiting for the opportunity to blackmail Jaci.

That could be dealt with. *Anything* could be dealt with, as long as Meech was still alive.

But the worst-case scenario breathed hot and heavy against the back of her neck, much too close for comfort.

Jaci stared at the mirror once more.

"Seriously, Meech. Where in the *literal* hell are you?"

The mirror cracked, a bright, jagged scar splitting the glass right down the middle.

Jaci laughed. "Add another seven years of bad luck to the epic shitshow of my life. Why not?"

Abandoning the bathroom, she headed for the kitchen and made some vanilla almond tea, trying to recalibrate.

The good news? She was still breathing, and she still had tea. As long as those two things held true, Jaci could figure out how to navigate the rest.

Unfortunately, "the rest" was a list long enough to fill a book.

For one thing, Viansa was topside, and it was only a matter of time before she unleashed her brand of hell on some poor, unsuspecting humans—not to mention the rest of the Redthornes. After she'd had her fill with all that, she'd undoubtedly come back for Jaci herself, the ultimate prize.

For another thing, Meech was MIA, very possibly dead. No, Jaci didn't want to believe it, but she didn't want to delude herself either. Viansa was incapable of mercy—Jaci knew that better than anyone. If she'd truly gotten her hands on Meech, it had likely ended badly.

Then there was the matter of her father. With Viansa in town, Jaci couldn't risk another visit to the hospital—not even a phone call to check on his status. Anything that might alert Viansa to the fact that Zachary Colburn was physically alive was officially off the table. She couldn't even *think* about the man again until Viansa was gone.

Jaci poured a splash of rum into the tea, then brought the mug to her lips, closing her eyes and inhaling the sweet, nutty scents. She took a sip and tried to steady her heartbeat, tried to ease the knots in her shoulders, tried to calm the burn in her stomach.

Nothing worked.

Because even with all the things threatening her very existence, with all the scenarios she'd played out, with all the fear and disappointments she'd already felt in the last few hours, Jaci knew the worst pain was yet to come.

Gabriel…

The dark wave of despair she'd been dutifully dodging all morning finally crashed over her in earnest, stealing her breath. She pressed a hand to her chest, suddenly feeling like the whole thing had just caved in on itself.

She'd fallen in love with a vampire prince. Her captor. Her savior. Her first kiss.

Seven *hells*, he'd changed her life with that kiss. Upended her entire world.

And then she'd upended his, every one of her lies and omissions suddenly forced to the surface. Every one of them slicing through him like a hot blade.

She'd seen it in his eyes long before he'd said the words, but it was the words themselves—the ice behind them—that haunted her now.

I will tolerate your presence as long as the task of eliminating your sister binds us. But the day I make a deal with a demon is the day you'll taste the last of my bitter ashes…

And it was all Jaci's fault. She never should've kept him in the dark. Never should've hidden her true nature.

Never should've let herself fall so hard, so deep for a man she might've just as easily—in another timeline, another life—murdered.

What the hell did she think would happen?

Let it go, girl. He's not coming back. Be grateful he left you instead of slaughtering your ass…

Footsteps outside the door startled her from her thoughts, making her drop the tea. The mug shattered at her feet. With no other weapon at hand, she grabbed the bottle of rum and headed out to face the intruder.

The door opened slowly, silently, keeping the person behind it in shadows.

But all the shadows in the world couldn't hide him from her heart.

Gabriel's wintergreen scent assaulted her senses, and she gasped, unshed tears blurring her vision. He finally stepped inside, stopping just over the threshold, letting the door close behind him with a *snick*.

A wave of emotion rose high in her throat, scraping her insides raw. Seeing him there, all rumple-haired and glassy-eyed, his shirt dark with old blood, his mouth set in a grim line…

Jaci ached to touch him. To feel the solid press of his body against hers, steadying her in the storm. Claiming her. Protecting her.

But all of that was gone, shattered in a foolish instant, and now she stared at him helplessly, knowing she'd never run her fingers through his thick hair, never taste the devastating sweetness of that kiss again...

She couldn't fucking breathe.

"Gabriel," she whispered. It was all she could manage—a name. A name that melted on her tongue and damn near obliterated her weary heart.

But all the vampire prince had to offer the witch he'd once so passionately claimed was ice.

He stood with his back rigid against the front door, arms crossed over his shoulders, gaze casting her in a deep freeze she felt all the way to her bones. There wasn't even hatred there. Hatred she could've dealt with, because it was still a feeling—a sign that some part of him, however deeply buried, still cared.

But Gabriel's eyes were distant, his face an impassive wall.

The only sign of any emotion at all was in the tight coil of his muscles, spring-loaded and ready to pounce.

To destroy.

"I've come here to end you, *witch*," he said coolly. "You've got three minutes to talk me out of it."

CHAPTER FOUR

It was a shite thing to say—harsh, cruel, pitiful. Gabriel knew it even before the words were out, but he'd spent the cold walk over to the apartment convincing himself he meant it, and he wasn't about to back down now.

No matter that the sight of her squeezed his heart like a fucking vise.

No matter that he still couldn't bring himself to hurt her.

No matter that he still, after everything, wanted to cover her lying mouth with his hand and fuck her until they both forgot they were ever supposed to hate each other in the first place.

"So that's what you're leading with, then?" Jacinda asked.

Gabriel didn't reply.

"I'm a big, bad bloodsucker and I've come here to end you," she mocked. "Honestly, Prince. I expected a little originality."

"Sarcasm? So that's *your* move?" Gabriel tsked. "I'm glad you find your imminent death amusing, but—"

"But you're here to end me. Yes, yes I understand." Jacinda shook her head, anger flashing in her eyes. Behind them, Gabriel saw a lifetime of pain and anguish and misery, all of it conspiring to mold the dark soul inside. "Do you know how many times I've heard that in my life?"

Bloody hell, how he longed to go to her. To fall to his knees and beg her to forgive him for all the things he said, for all the times he threatened her, for all the ways he didn't —*couldn't*—save her.

His leg muscles twitched, already imagining his feet moving across the floor—three steps to close the distance. Three steps to gather her into his arms, press his lips to her ear, and whisper all the secrets he'd kept locked inside, too afraid to let them out in the open.

But Gabriel knew he couldn't. Loving Jacinda Colburn was a foolish fantasy—it always had been.

"Considering you're still breathing?" he said instead, folding his arms across his chest and offering a casual shrug. "Not nearly enough."

"Oh yeah? Say it again, then," she taunted, gripping her bottle of booze like a weapon. "Say it again!"

His cock stiffened at the fire in her voice, flooding his mind with memories of her warm body pinned beneath him, writhing against him, begging him for more.

Desire simmered inside, but Gabriel ignored it. "After everything you've done, *witch*, it's no less than you deserve."

"Deserve *this*, dickhead!" She pitched the bottle at him, narrowly missing his head. It struck the door behind him, exploding in an unexpected burst of light and heat.

Gabriel spun around, instinctively ducking to avoid the wild, silver-blue sunburst.

It could only be one thing.

Hellfire.

He watched, mesmerized, terrified, fucking *awed* by its otherworldly beauty as it crept up the door and licked at the ceiling. It seemed to be eating the very air but left no damage in its path, no blackened plaster or blistering paint.

Across the room, Jacinda stood with her hands raised, her lush mouth parted, eyes shining with the barest hint of the dark power he'd seen in the water last night. Flames roiled and churned at her command, following a liquid path across the ceiling, straight back to the witch-demon.

Hellfire rained down upon her shoulders, flame by flame, vanishing beneath her skin until there wasn't a single trace of it left. She lowered her head and met Gabriel's gaze, the last of the silver-blue hellfire flickering in her eyes, then fading.

It was horrifying. It was beautiful. And in that moment, Gabriel had never feared her more.

Never *wanted* her more, either, and there was that damned devil on his shoulder again, pushing him in the wrong fucking direction.

He stalked toward her. One step, two, three, just like he'd counted in his head, and then he had her backed up and pinned against the glass balcony doors, no escape.

Not unless she wanted to incinerate him.

She pressed her hands against his chest, her touch warm and defiant, the threat in her eyes clear.

"Do it," he dared, half wishing she would. Half wishing she'd end this fucking nightmare existence once and for all. "Light me up, little moonflower. Watch me *burn*."

He felt the heat gathering in her hands. Felt it radiating through his blood-stained shirt. His skin.

Deep in his lungs, the first ember caught. Smoldered. Made his eyes water.

"Do it," he whispered hoarsely, barely holding back a cough. "Fucking do it."

She quirked an elegant eyebrow.

He wondered if it would be quick. Wondered if it would hurt. Wondered if she'd be waiting for him on the other side of hell.

But Jacinda wouldn't give him the chance to find out.

She dropped her hands, clenching them into fists at her sides. The heat dissipated, leaving nothing but the faint taste of smoke and brimstone in his mouth.

Gabriel grabbed her jaw, tilted her face up. Forced her to meet his gaze.

"Make your move, dickhead," she practically hissed. "My three minutes are up."

"You're not even going to try to explain yourself?"

"Why? Nothing I say will make a damn bit of difference. You made that quite clear with your little speech this morning—you don't trust me."

"And why the fuck should I?"

"Because I… You're…" She tried valiantly to hold on to her righteous anger, but it dimmed as swiftly as the hellfire, her eyes welling with tears, all the sharp edges of her voice turning soft. "I'm sorry. I never meant… I wanted to tell you about Viansa's connection to the curse, but there was never a right time, and everything last night happened so fast…"

"You're sorry? That's it? Sorry you lied about your sister and the curse? Sorry you forgot to tell me you're part demon? Sorry a dangerous succubus is loose in a city of nine million humans, not to mention countless supernaturals, every one of them at risk? Sorry you planned to kill me, resurrect me, and leave me trapped in a life of misery as a fucking mindless gray?"

"I'm sorry for all of it."

"Sorry," he repeated, as if it were a foreign word whose translation he just couldn't grasp, no matter how many times he heard it.

"More than you know, Prince."

Still gripping her jaw, Gabriel brought his mouth close to hers. Did everything in his fucking power to ignore the taste of her cloves-and-cinnamon breath, the memory of her kiss, the dark craving clawing through his chest, kicking his heart into overdrive.

The red dress from last night still clung to her curves, and the sight of it sent him right back to the boathouse. His other hand clenched tight, itching to touch the fabric again. To push it up to her waist, exposing her thighs. To pull her close and fuck her hot and hard against the wall, just as he

SARAH PIPER

had in that boathouse, until they cracked the plaster and chased off every last doubt festering between them.

Gabriel released her jaw and dragged his thumb across her lips, mesmerized by their soft, pillowy feel. By the hitch in her breath. By the light in her eyes.

All of it made his heart ache.

"Why?" he whispered.

"I told you," she said. "Everything happened so fast. When I woke up this morning, I promised myself I'd come clean about—"

He shook his head, cutting her off and drawing even closer to her mouth. "Why did you let me kiss you?"

Fucking hell, the look in her eyes nearly gutted him. It was the kind of look that could lead a man to his death, and Gabriel was five seconds from following her right over the cliff.

Her lips curved into the softest smile, warm breath ghosting across his thumb.

"Because for all your threats and tough-guy bullshit," she said, "you're the first vampire I've ever felt safe with."

Gabriel tried to force out a laugh, but all he managed was a sad little huff. "*That* was your first fuckup."

"It wasn't a fuckup."

"Then it's willful ignorance, which is even worse." He lowered his hand and turned his back on her, desperate to break their intense connection before the last of his anger abandoned him. "I've told you, witch. I'm not your white knight."

"And I'm not some damsel in distress waiting on a

42

fucking fairy tale, so you can take that white knight bullshit and shove it up your arrogant ass. Do you really think that's why I let you kiss—"

"Arrogant ass?" He spun around to face her again, the air between them crackling with electric heat. "You've got *some* nerve speaking to me that way, considering what you did."

"*Me*? You came here, into *my* home, and threatened to kill me!"

"This is *my* home, witch. And you nearly got us both killed this morning with that sister of yours—a secret that's about to destroy a lot of innocent lives."

"And I said I was sorry. So we can either move forward from there and talk about how to stop Viansa, or you can do what you came here to do and send me to hell in peace."

"Oh, you'd love that, wouldn't you? Martyring yourself, leaving the rest of us to clean up your mess." Gabriel scrubbed a hand over his jaw, his hatred for her deepening by the minute. "I bloody *despise* demons."

"Good," she snapped. "I bloody *despise* vampires. Way worse than hellspawn *any* day of the week."

"Is that so?"

She folded her arms across her chest, defiant as ever. "Damn straight."

"So you're telling me you'd rather I killed a few of my own instead of Chernikov's mutts? Instead of the bastard whose tongue I ripped out this morning just for sending you into a death trap?"

"You… what?" Her eyes widened, and she reached for him, trailing her fingers along his blood-stained shirt.

But Gabriel didn't want her touch. Didn't want to see that fucking look in her eyes again.

He ripped open the shirt and shucked it off, tossing it to the ground with a snarl of disgust. "I've bathed in more blood on your account in two months than I have in my entire life as a vampire."

"I'd say thanks, but if your hero complex gets any bigger—"

"Yes, and we all know how much you appreciate being saved."

Her gaze burned hot again, then dimmed, a cascade of unbidden tears rushing down her cheeks. She swiped at them hastily, her anger rising right alongside his. "Say what you want about the demons who hurt me, but there's one thing worse than a monster who brutalizes women for fun, Gabriel. And that's a monster who sanctions it. A monster who trades favors, using a woman as currency. A monster who offers up a woman like a piece of property to buy or sell or give away, just because he woke up that morning with a burning desire to impress some rich scumbag. You want to hate demons? Fine. Be my guest. But let's not pretend *your* kind aren't the ones sitting at the top of that fucked-up supernatural food chain, bloodsucker."

"You're talking about Duchanes," he said. It wasn't a question, and Jacinda didn't answer. She didn't need to.

Images of Duchanes flashed behind Gabriel's eyes—his smarmy smile, his meaty hand on Jacinda's lower back the night of Dorian's fundraiser. Even then, Gabriel could see how much the vampire repulsed her—and that was just from the thirty-second public display Duchanes had put on. He couldn't even imagine what it'd been like for her at home, when all Duchanes' servants had taken their leave and the doors were shut tight against prying eyes.

Guilt knifed through his gut, mixing with a white-hot rage that burned only for Renault Duchanes.

"Why didn't you kill him?" he demanded. "You're a bloody demon, for fuck's sake. You could've lit his ass up with that hellfire and ended your troubles in an instant."

"And become House Duchanes' Most Wanted? No way. Besides, I needed the job."

"A job. Of course. So you had to sign on with a vampire house? No one in this town looking for a perky little barista?"

"Last time I checked, Starbucks wasn't offering free room and board, unrestricted access to magical tools and research, and the perfect cover for messing around with spells all day." She closed her eyes and blew out a heavy breath. "Look. Someone I love *very* much was in danger. *Is* in danger. I knew I could help my father, but I needed time to figure out the right spells. Without realizing it, Duchanes gave me that—for a few years, anyway."

"So all that suffering, all that cruelty—"

"Was a small price to pay in exchange for a chance at saving my father's soul." At this, she opened her eyes, pinning him in place with her steely gaze. "And I'm sorry you don't understand that—I'm sorry your father was such a terrible bastard. Truly I am. But mine wasn't. *Isn't*. He's kind and loving, he's got a wicked sense of humor, he never stopped looking out for me, and ever since I got to New York, I've fucking *lived* for the day when I can bring him back. When I can leave all this supernatural shit behind and make a life with him outside the prison of hell and the tortures of my so-called family. And I get that you're pissed at me—I deserve your anger, your threats, whatever punishments you want to throw at me. But as long as I'm still alive, if you think for one second I'm going to let you stand in the way of helping my dad, I swear to every devil in hell, Gabriel Redthorne. I will—"

Gabriel blurred into her space, capturing her in his arms and holding her tight against his chest, making her gasp.

He couldn't do it any longer. Couldn't stay away from her, couldn't hold onto his anger, couldn't even follow the rational line of his arguments. Every damn one of them led back to her soft mouth. Back to the kiss and every dark, devious promise it held.

"You'll *what*, little moonflower?" he whispered. "Tell me. Tell me all the terrible, menacing things you'll do to the vampire who dares to cross you."

She remained silent, panting in his grasp, her heart fluttering like a bird in a cage.

"Nothing to say? Hmm." Gabriel buried his face in the crook of her neck, inhaling deeply, slowly dragging his mouth up to her ear. "Then allow me to tell you all the terrible, menacing things the vampire is going to do to *you*."

CHAPTER FIVE

"I own you," Gabriel murmured, fangs slicing through his gums as he dragged his mouth back down along her neck. "Everything about you belongs to me. I told you that from the start, did I not?"

"Yes," Jacinda breathed, her heart still thrumming, the scent of her fear mingling with the scent of her raw, unchecked desire. "You... you did."

"But all this time, it was you, laying your claim on *me*. Trapping me in your web of schemes and lies." He finally gave in to the desperate urge to touch her dress, gathering the fabric in his fist, exposing her knees, her bare thighs, the scrap of lace between them.

His fingers brushed along the top edge of her panties, making her tremble.

"So I'll ask you, little moonflower, one more time." He slid his fingers behind the lace, dipping lower, lower still. "Who owns this pussy?"

"You, Gabriel. Only you."

"Are you certain?"

"I swear it. It's yours, Gabriel. It's—oh, *fuck*..." She trailed off into a sigh as he grazed her clit, then slid two fingers inside her. She was already so wet for him, her flesh hot and slick, everything about her making him weak.

Her pulse pounded beneath the pale skin of her throat, a matching throb of desire echoing in his fangs. Killing her would be easy. Pleasurable. Devastating.

"And my heart?" he asked, one hand tangling in the hair at the base of her neck as he thrust deeper inside, a slow, torturous stroke that left her gasping. "Do I own that as well, or are you still planning to carve it out of my chest?"

Jacinda's hands tightened around his shoulders, her legs parting to give him more access, her body begging for his touch.

Deeper. Harder. More.

He gave in to her demands, powerless against the siren call of her desire, claiming her flesh with every stroke.

"No," she panted. "I wasn't going to go through with it. I... I never could. I... Gabriel, that's... Don't stop..."

But he did stop, fingers stilling inside her, relishing in the hot the pulse of her body as he denied her the release she was so close to finding.

"Please," she whispered. "I need you to touch me."

"What about what *I* need, little moonflower?" He drew her closer, his mouth just a hair's breadth from hers, the warmth of her breath stirring him, making his mouth water. He grazed her lips with his fangs, and she shivered, a delicious tremble he felt all the way down between her thighs.

"What… what do you need?" she asked.

Truly, Gabriel needed to make her come. To prove to himself that he still had some semblance of control in a situation that had spun so far out of his grasp, he could barely remember how it'd all begun.

He pulled out of her wet heat, dragging his fingers over her clit, teasing her, bringing her close once more before sliding back inside. Slow. Deep. A game of exquisite torture that left her panting and crazed.

"You're in luck," he replied softly. "On this, our interests are *blissfully* aligned. I need to touch you, little moonflower. I need to hear the sounds of your ecstasy as I make you burn for me."

With every word, he thrust in deeper, faster, increasing the pressure and intensity until he brought her right back to the precipice again.

Then he stopped.

"Oh, God," she breathed. "I can't take it."

"You can. You *will*, because this pussy is mine to do with as I please. Isn't that what you said?"

"I… yes." Jacinda was holding on by a thread, her words a faint whisper, her cheeks dark, blood rushing through her veins in a way that damn near hypnotized him.

Gabriel released her hair and took her face in his hand, tracing the outline of her lips with his thumb.

"But what of this mouth?" he whispered, nipping her

earlobe. "Is it still mine to kiss? Mine to fuck? Mine to do with as I please?"

"It's yours, Gabriel. All of it. I—oh, *fuck*..."

He thrust deep inside her once more, curling his fingers as he rocked his palm against her clit, stroking and rubbing and fucking her, inhaling her sweet breath as she panted and begged.

"Gabriel! I'm right there! It's... fuck... Don't stop!"

"That's it, little moonflower. Beg for it. Show me how badly you need to be touched."

"Please!" she cried out, riding his hand, matching every thrust, her body quivering, and then...

"*Come*," he commanded, hitting the perfect spot, holding her close as she melted for him, writhing and panting, gasping, shattering.

The moment it was over, he slid his fingers out of her panties and shoved them into her mouth, issuing another command. "Suck."

On a desperate moan, she obeyed, the hot silk of her tongue sliding over his skin, her gaze locked on his in a fierce battle of wills. Of desire.

Fisting her hair again, he leaned in close to that eager mouth and whispered, "Tell me to stop, Jacinda Colburn."

The accursed witch merely shook her head.

Gabriel yanked his fingers free and claimed her in a suffocating kiss, the taste of her own desire fresh on her tongue. She tasted like the sea, like her own wild, untamed magic, and in a blinding instant he was right back in the ocean again, desperate to save her. To protect her. To make her his.

The kiss turned fierce, bruising, both of them fighting for dominance. When they finally broke for air, she dropped suddenly to her knees, raking her fingernails down his chest, scoring his flesh, *scorching* it. Her touch was so hot, so all-consuming, Gabriel swore he'd look down and find a trail of hellfire.

But there were only scratches, his skin welling with blood, then healing just as quickly.

Gabriel reached for her face with both hands, tilting her toward him. Darkness swirled in her eyes, another hint of what he'd seen last night at the beach, calling to the darkness that roiled inside him, never far from the surface. She licked her lips and reached for his cock, palming his erection with one hand as she tried frantically to unbutton his pants.

"Jacinda…" he whispered, rolling his head back, shivering with anticipation. With need.

Urgent fingers finally freed that blasted button. Unzipped the zipper. Unleashed his aching cock and gripped him with a firm, red-hot touch he'd missed more than he'd realized.

But then he made the mistake of looking at her again. Of meeting those eyes. The dark soul behind them.

And the truth, however damned inconvenient, broke into his mind once more.

A half demon hybrid bred to destroy him.

A sister ready to lay waste to the city.

A curse he was no closer to breaking.

And a thousand secrets and lies conspiring to shatter his heart, figuratively and literally both.

Gabriel had already given in to the desire to make her come, and now he wanted nothing more than her touch. Her mouth. Her nails drawing blood, her hellfire consuming him as he succumbed to the darkness and fucked her until neither of them could breathe.

But Jacinda Colburn was his weakness. If he didn't stop now, she'd be his complete undoing—a risk he couldn't take. Not while his brothers were counting on him to make this right.

He grabbed her wrist, twisting her hand away.

Confusion clouded her eyes.

"Let me touch you," she whispered, close enough that he could feel the mist of her breath on his cock, warm and wet and full of promise.

He released her wrist and dragged the back of his hand across his mouth, trying to obliterate the taste of her. Failing. He was utterly *full* of her—those blue eyes, the scent of her, the raw ocean-salt of her desire still lingering on his tongue...

Gabriel closed his eyes and shook his head, tucking himself back into his pants. His heart seized up again, a painfully sharp ache echoing through his entire being.

One he couldn't afford to reveal. Not to her. Not even to himself.

For the vampire and his devious witch-demon, this interlude wasn't a reunion.

It was a goodbye.

When he opened his eyes again, he found her still on her knees, still blinking up at him, her hand half-raised as if he might just change his mind and finally give in to the pleasure of her touch.

It wouldn't take much convincing.

So Gabriel thought of his brothers. Of Isabelle. Of all the people counting on him to finally, for once in his reckless life, do the right fucking thing.

Then he grabbed her hands, pulled her to her feet, and said the one thing *guaranteed* to put those searing blue eyes on ice. "I'd *much* rather talk about your sister."

CHAPTER SIX

After twenty minutes beneath a just-south-of-scalding-hot shower, Jaci's experiment came to a disappointing end.

The verdict?

Nope, not even an entire bottle of expensive luxury body wash—*with* exfoliating pearls and extra moisturizers made from the tears of baby wombats or something—could wash away the touch of that infuriating vampire prince.

She was shocked—and the tiniest bit grateful—he'd even allowed her a few minutes alone in the bathroom, given the murderous rage still flashing in his eyes after he'd hauled her up off the floor. But she wasn't stupid enough to think he'd let her hang out all day, sudsing away her many sins.

And by sins, she meant him.

Even when he wanted to kill her, his touch was electrifying. Captivating. And if she spent any more time contemplating all the myriad ways she wanted him to make her come—to *command* her, body and soul—she'd probably end up popping off a burst of accidental hellfire and incinerating herself.

So after the shower and a quick change into her reliable sweats-and-spandex combo, she emerged from the bathroom determined to stay on task.

Viansa.

This time, Jaci would cover all the bases: who the succubus was, how she operated, what she wanted.

And most importantly, how to take her ass down.

It was all about the mission now—no room for screwing around with petty things like feelings or orgasms, or feelings *about* orgasms, or orgasms that felt like—

Knock it off, asshole. Get yourself a giant fucking vibrator, name it Vlad the Impaler, and buzz-buzz-buzz away every last memory of that sexy, arrogant vampire prince. Problem solved!

With a devilish smirk, Jaci made a mental note to charge a few new toys of the battery-operated nature to Gabriel's credit card, twisted her damp hair into a bun, then marched into the living room to face the music.

Gabriel must've taken a detour up to his place because he'd obviously showered and changed too, damp hair curling at the base of his neck, a dark gray Henley stretched across his broad shoulders, perfectly distressed jeans hanging just low enough on his hips not to be obnoxious. His feet were bare, which shouldn't have been so sexy, but... *damn.* Bare feet were intimate. They were the jeans-pulled-on-after-morning-sex, let-the-dog-out, let's-make-brunch-and-then-have-sex-again kind of intimate she hadn't even realized she'd longed for until that very moment, seeing his toes against the hardwood floor, the shadow of his ankle bone, the casual everyday-ness of a thing she'd never be able to have.

Forcing her gaze away from his feet, Jaci lingered again on the space where his shirt met his belt line. Despite her big plans for Vlad, it still took everything in her not to drop to her knees again and beg the stupid vampire to let her run her tongue along the drool-worthy v-shaped muscles she knew lurked just behind that clothing…

"Dinner?" Gabriel asked, breaking into her naughty thoughts. "Or would you rather keep staring at my cock?"

"What? I wasn't staring at… at *it*. I was… um… Did you say something about dinner?" She forced a smile, even though the bright-red burn in her cheeks was all the evidence the smug bastard needed to convict her of the crime of being obsessed with him. And his cock. "Are you cooking?"

With a smirk she couldn't help but adore, he waved a menu at her—the one from the empanada place around the corner. She hadn't even noticed he'd been holding it.

Because she was too busy staring at his cock.

And his feet.

And the way that shirt stretched so perfectly over his torso, outlining every dip and curve of those muscles…

"Fine, but you're buying," she said, sidestepping him as she headed into the kitchen. "I'll make drinks. Hey, speaking of which… Am I on the schedule tonight?"

It was a loaded question, but one she suddenly needed an answer to. He hadn't murdered her yet, so there was still a chance she had a job. And if she was still gainfully—though somewhat unconventionally—employed, the last thing she wanted to do was miss her shift and piss off the boss who'd already threatened to kill her once today.

"No," he said. Then, with another cocky smirk she wanted to slap, or possibly kiss, or possibly slap while kissing, "I've decided to close the club tonight. We'll open again tomorrow, but you're not going back on the schedule until we've got this Viansa situation figured out."

"Fair enough," she said, trying hard not to show her relief.

The whole thing was insane. *She* was insane. Two months ago, when he'd first given her an apron and an ultimatum, the last thing she wanted to do was become some scantily clad barmaid slinging cocktails for Gabriel and his asshole friends.

Now, she couldn't imagine *not* working at Obsidian. Not working for him.

Funny what a difference a couple of months—and falling in love—made.

Not that it mattered now.

Jaci blew out a breath, blinking away tears. Their partnership, as he'd so clearly pointed out this morning, was nothing more than an arrangement now. A mission.

Track down the succubus. Break the curse. Send the bitch back to hell. Roll the credits.

Food ordered and drinks sufficiently mixed, they were

all out of stalling tactics. So, with nothing more to lose but the last shreds of her pride and privacy, Jaci took a fortifying gulp of her Magical Mint Julep, met the vampire's intense, forest-green gaze, and waded into the shark-infested waters of her past.

CHAPTER SEVEN

"Succubi manifest in human dreams," Jaci said, "for the sole purpose of getting laid."

Gabriel flashed that smirk again, sending a little zing to her stomach. "And here I thought it was to tempt the innocents to sin."

"Tempt them to *come*, would be a more accurate way of describing it. The sin part was added in later—mankind's way of passing judgment."

"Typical."

Jaci nodded, taking another sip of her drink. "The end goal is always pregnancy, and they use every trick in their arsenal. Mental manipulation, erotic dream creation, fear. Sometimes they want their victims to impregnate them directly, but usually, they just collect the… you know. And bring it back to hell."

"No, Jacinda. I actually don't know anything about this,

which is why we're in this predicament. If I *had* known, I would've found a way to divert this train wreck before—"

"Ejaculate," she blurted out, feeling like a kid caught with porn. She gulped down some more booze, wishing it would cool the burn in her cheeks. "They collect it and use it to breed demon-human hybrids in hell."

"For what purpose? Aren't other demons more powerful than humans? Why would they essentially water down their line like that?"

"It's a best-of-both worlds kind of thing. The offspring are usually immortal, with demonic powers, but have an easier time passing between realms than other demons. They have their own forms and don't need to possess human vessels. They can basically live as humans on earth, undetected by the other supernatural races, which means they're not bound by your Shadow Accords."

"Great. So they don't have to follow our rules about territories and age restrictions on demon deals." Gabriel sighed and sipped his drink, trying not to wince.

Jaci hid her smile, recalling the first time she'd made him a drink, right before he'd put her to work at Obsidian. He'd practically swayed that day too. Just like now.

Still can't handle my magical cocktails, huh, Prince?

"They don't have to follow *anyone's* rules," she said, chasing away the old memory before it got her into trouble. "Some of them live completely human lives, never getting involved in supernatural politics. Others live among the demons here, enjoying the privilege of their anonymity in the human world, using that to curry favor with guys like

Chernikov and Rogozin. A few of them form their own communities, though you'd never know it if you ran into them on the street."

"Would you?"

"Only if I'd seen them in hell first."

"How dangerous are they?"

"That's the thing, Prince. No matter which path they choose to walk on earth, at their core, they're *always* loyal to hell—first and foremost."

"Like demonic sleeper cells," Gabriel said, and Jaci nodded.

"An army already in place, awaiting the call."

"Why hasn't it come?"

"The most powerful demons—ones like my mother and sister—are hellbound. Viansa's sudden jailbreak aside, there just aren't enough of the O.G. demons here to wage any kind of war. It wouldn't make sense to risk exposing the hybrids for a war they had no chance at winning."

"But if someone breaks the gates, and all those originals find a way to manifest here, the odds shift in their favor."

"Exactly. Because at that point, why bother with demon deals and human vessels if you can just bring all the worst, most badass, most unbreakable demons up from the source? You'd have them, plus the hybrids already in place... No contest."

"And this is what Viansa's planning?"

"I think so. Whether it's possible is another story."

The delivery guy arrived, so while Gabriel dealt with the food, Jaci scooted into the kitchen to make another round of drinks. She passed him some plates and silverware first, and by the time she returned with fresh Magical Mint Juleps in hand, Gabriel had everything spread out on the table, gesturing for her to take a seat and dig in.

For one ridiculous moment, it almost felt like a real date.

The thought made her chest constrict, and she forced down a drink to loosen the sudden tightness in her throat.

After they'd each eaten a couple of empanadas, Gabriel said, "Back to the succubi and the dream thing. Is that how you were conceived? Some poor bloke's wet dream?"

Jaci shot him a murderous glare. "Watch it, dickhead. The poor bloke you're speaking of is my father."

He had the grace to lower his eyes, but that was as close to an apology as she was going to get.

She reached for the last ham-and-cheese empanada—the one she'd noticed was his favorite—and stole it from right under his nose.

Good. Serves him right.

"No," she finally said, tempering her frustration. "That's not how I was conceived. My mother isn't a succubus— Viansa gets that particular trait from her father."

"An incubus?"

"The original."

"And your mother?" Noticing the missing ham-and-cheese, he sighed and helped himself to a spinach empanada instead. "What sort of demon is she?"

"She's… harder to categorize. She doesn't appear in dreams, but she *can* be summoned, which is how my father met her."

Jaci told him the story, just as her father had told her when she was old enough to understand.

He was only in his twenties when he first met her, but already a powerful dark mage, his skills and intuition surpassing most of his coven members, including the elders. More and more, he began practicing on his own, experimenting with riskier spells, pushing the boundaries, calling upon darker powers.

"He learned to summon and bind original demons," she explained, "which meant he could channel some of their power without ceding control of his mind and body. In exchange, he made offerings to them, granted favors, that sort of thing."

"Why? If he could bind them, why not just take what he needed, no payment required?"

"Balance. Give and take, he always said. A one-sided deal, no matter how tempting at the time, always comes back to bite you in the end." She shook her head, a familiar ache forming in the pit of her stomach. "Unfortunately for my father, it came back to bite him anyway."

Jaci set aside her half-eaten empanada, opting for more liquid courage instead. This was the part she'd been dreading. The part where all the landmines lie buried, waiting for her to step on them and blow herself to bits.

"My father was a good man," she said. "A good mage. His only fault was falling for the charms of a beautiful demon."

"That makes two of us," Gabriel grumbled, but when

Jaci looked up to meet his eyes, he quickly waved away the words. "Please. Continue."

"He summoned my mother often, not realizing how powerful she truly was. Each time she came to him, she made him feel stronger, more in tune with his magic, like he could do literally anything. In turn, she was siphoning his power too. His judgment. She couldn't manifest outside of the summoning circle, but eventually, after several summonings, she finally convinced my father to follow her back home."

"To hell," Gabriel clarified, and Jaci nodded. "How is that possible for a living being?"

"The dead don't have a monopoly on traveling to hell. The living can go too, but most don't. It's too dangerous, and nearly impossible to find your way back out."

"Your father went anyway, though? Even knowing the risks?"

"He believed he was in love." She sipped her drink, waiting for it to chase off the prickly heat that'd crept over her skin. "The moment he stepped through the hell gate, he knew he'd made a terrible mistake. But by then it was too late."

She told him the rest of her father's story—the details he was willing to share, anyway. How her mother—with help from her precious Viansa—drugged him, tortured him, and forced him to impregnate her before an audience of original demons.

"Originals have their own magic," she explained. "During the ritual, they raised their communal power, allowing my mother to channel all of their combined dark energy into this one act, this one perfect outcome." A hot tear slid down Jaci's cheek, and she let it fall, too ashamed to even brush it away. "But it turns out I wasn't so perfect after all."

Gabriel let out a slow, steady breath. Before she even realized what was happening, he reached across the table, covering her hand with his, holding her tight.

He didn't say a word. Just held her hand, his thumb skating over her knuckles, his eyes losing some of their frost.

Bolstered by the unexpected show of support, Jaci continued.

"I was supposed to be the first of a new breed. My mother and sister believed they could somehow merge the dark, destructive powers of hell with the creative magic of a powerful human mage, creating a demon even stronger and more useful than the half-human hybrids the succubi made. One that could not only travel between realms, but could practice *true* magic, channeling power from both realms, bending the very fabric of reality to her will. To my mother and sister's will."

"You said you were bred to destroy vampires," he said. "How does that come into play?"

"Up here, in the so-called human realm, vampires control the supernatural world—your family in particular. Your brother might feel like he's barely got a grip, but the truth is, vampire control runs much deeper than politics, and is a much older and more formidable power than the reign of a single royal bloodline. Your very existence keeps the supernatural world spinning."

"I don't understand. Witches created vampires. It's the only reason we exist."

"Yes, they did create you. And shifters. But now, without you, the whole thing falls apart."

"Why?"

"Witches created you. And witch magic keeps you from turning into the grays. But vampire blood magic also fuels the witches and mages themselves, who in turn control the hell portals, balancing the flow of demonic essences and other non-human entities into this realm. It's a complex, symbiotic, and highly evolved system with vampires being the most integral part. Eliminate you, and the rest of the dominoes quickly fall, clearing the way for demons to rule the world. Or enslave it. Or burn it down—whatever they want. So, with a combination of hellfire and magic—the darkest magic you can imagine—even just a handful of hybrids like me, working in concert and in secret, could take down your entire race. It would take a long time, but yes, it could absolutely be done, and that's precisely what my family envisioned."

"Yet you *haven't* taken us down," he said, releasing her hand and leaning back in his chair, a bit of the frost returning to his eyes. "Why?"

"I told you, I wasn't the perfect specimen they'd hoped for. Not for lack of trying—all I ever wanted to do was please them. I jumped through every hoop, sat through every experiment..." Jaci fought off a shiver, her old ghosts never far. "All the things I told you about this morning are true, Gabriel. It was torture. Absolute torture. And in the end, I showed no sign of the dark demonic powers I was supposed to manifest. No indication I could do anything more than cast a bit of hellfire and craft a few spells."

"Are there others?" he asked, and she knew by the way he watched her—the distrust in his eyes, the wariness around the edges—he wasn't asking about original demons like her mother and sister.

He was asking about *her*.

"Not that I'm aware of." Jaci sipped her drink. "When I turned out to be such an epic disappointment, I'm pretty sure they put that experiment on the shelf and moved on."

"That doesn't mean they aren't working on others. Something even more dangerous and deadly."

Jaci shrugged. "Hell is full of experiments. My mother is just one demon, my sister another, both bent on global human and supernatural domination, just like all the rest. Half the time they're teaming up, the other half they're trying to kill each other, because that's how original demons roll. So yeah, you asked if there's something even more dangerous? Bet on it, Prince. It could literally be anything."

Gabriel ran his thumb along his lower lip, calling her attention to his sexy-as-sin mouth. Holy hell, what that mouth had done to her…

Thankfully, before she could fall headlong into another fantasy, he lowered his hand and said, "Tell me about the night they released you. You said your father made some sort of bargain?"

"When I turned eighteen and still hadn't made significant progress, instead of killing me outright like she'd threatened, my mother decided to give me one last chance to prove my worthiness. She and Viansa made an elaborate game of it, inviting the originals who'd witnessed my conception, turning the whole thing into a festival. I was led into a gladiator arena, forced to fight seven different demons. My mother promised me that if I could defeat them all, she'd set my father free."

"But not you?"

Jaci shook her head. "Only him. I was sentenced to death either way. I figured I had nothing to lose—I'd either die at the hand of one of the seven demons, or I'd die at the hands of my sister and mother. I just wanted a chance for Dad to have a life. He'd spent those eighteen years in hell as a prisoner, still doing his best to keep me safe from all the monsters, to keep us away from the most dangerous hell realms, to help me avoid the worst of the abuses and comfort me when I couldn't."

"And your father allowed this... this deathmatch to proceed?"

"He fought her on it, of course, but he had no power against my mother. In the end, it didn't matter anyway. Miraculously, I defeated six demons, but the seventh was a high-level fire demon I just didn't have the skills to outsmart. He would've incinerated me, but my mother stepped in at the last second and slaughtered him, lording it over me like she'd done me an epic favor."

"She saved you," he said grimly, "just so she could kill you later?"

"More fun for her that way, I suppose. But then my father came through with another deal—the offer of a lifetime." Jaci sucked in another gulp of her drink, then forced out the words. "His soul for my freedom."

"But… why would she take the deal? She already owned both of you, and you'd lost against the demon. His soul was already hers."

"My father was an unwilling captive. He resisted her at every turn—always had, even through the haze of drugs and torture. She and Viansa often wondered if his resistance was the reason I was such a failure. Like, the ritual didn't work because he was actively channeling his powers to break it. With this deal, though, he was offering himself freely—the worst demon deal a person could sign. She'd have complete dominion over his soul, his will, his magic, all of it. No, he didn't hold a candle to her hell magic, but he was still an extremely powerful dark mage. In her eyes, it really *was* the offer of a lifetime. What did she care if I went topside? I was useless to her at that point, and she and Viansa both knew that without him, I'd be dead in a week.

"Dad was allowed to escort me through the portal. We came to New York City—deposited in an empty alley in Little Italy. I still remember the smell of the food—so rich and spicy and like nothing I'd ever smelled before. It was wintertime, like it is now—I'd never felt true cold before. I remember gazing up into the night sky and wondering why the stars were falling. 'It's snow, baby,' he said, tears in his eyes like it was the most miraculous thing ever. The two of us laughed, spinning in circles, holding out our hands and catching snowflakes. For those first few minutes, I think we both believed we'd escaped together. That the nightmare was over."

Jaci had never told anyone the full story before. For seven long years, it had existed only in her dreams—the best and the worst of them. And though the tears fell unbidden now, the memories slicing through her ribcage and cutting deep gouges in her heart, the thing she felt most of all was... relief.

Relief that it was no longer a secret. Relief that someone —even a vampire prince who might still kill her at the end of it—had listened.

"One minute he was laughing and smiling," she continued, "and the next, he collapsed in my arms, his breathing turning shallow. I screamed for him not to leave me, tears nearly freezing on my cheeks, but I knew exactly what was happening. He was dying. My mother was cashing in on their deal. I felt the tug of his soul as it escaped his body, and suddenly I just... I knew, Gabriel. I knew my mother was wrong."

"How do you mean?"

"She always believed the darkest powers of hell had somehow skipped over me. But in that heartbeat of a moment, while my father died in my arms and his soul left his body, I knew with utter certainty that *that* one—the *most* powerful one, the darkest and most dangerous—had *not* skipped me."

He leaned forward in his chair, eyes full of wonder and revulsion both, capturing her in a gaze she couldn't look away from even if she'd wanted to.

In a whisper so soft she had to read it on his lips to understand, he said, "Which power, Jacinda?"

The admission, she realized, would confirm his worst thoughts about her. All the things he'd accused her of but couldn't prove. The vile, repulsive things that would drive that final stake into the heart of whatever they'd once meant to each other.

In this city, witch, death is a kindness. That you'd seek to defy it is nothing less than madness...

He'd said it to her on their first meeting at Bloodbath, right after the attack.

Even then, she hadn't outright admitted it, preferring to let him draw his own conclusions.

This morning, in the wake of Viansa's dramatic exit from the penthouse, she'd told him that she'd brought her father back.

But she still hadn't said the real word. The *true* word. Not like this.

Up until now, Gabriel might've thought she'd been speaking in metaphor. Might've thought she'd brought her father back the way a paramedic brings back a drowning victim with chest compressions and CPR. Might've even missed that part of her story entirely—that's how angry he was.

But as much as she wished she could keep this *one* thing unspoken between them, this one last secret all to herself, Jaci knew there was no going back now.

Vita mutatur, non tollitur.

Life is changed, not taken away.

Blood on the roses. Blood on the sheets. Blood on the snow. Blood on the grave.

The dead shall rise. The dead shall return.

"The power," she said softly, forcing herself to hold his gaze, "of necromancy."

CHAPTER EIGHT

It was a long time before her vampire prince spoke again, and though Jaci was about ready to jump through the damn balcony doors to escape his dark, penetrating gaze, she forced herself to remain still. She didn't even risk the movement it would take to bring the drink to her lips, though she desperately, *desperately* wanted to.

Beyond those beautiful glass doors, a full moon rose high in a clear sky, casting the surrounding buildings in an otherworldly light that made her confession feel that much more ominous.

Finally, when she couldn't take another agonizing minute of his silent scrutiny, she whispered, "Please tell me what you're thinking, Gabriel. Whatever it is, I can handle it. Just… don't give me the silent treatment. Not now."

Gabriel nodded slowly, still trying to process everything she'd told him. He sipped his drink, then sipped it again.

"For all the monstrous things I've seen," he finally said,

"the monstrous things I've done…" He closed his eyes and shook his head. "There's a darkness in you that bloody terrifies me, Jacinda Colburn."

"I know," she said softly. "My whole life, I just wanted to be normal. I *still* want to be normal."

It was a small confession, but it felt big to say it out loud. Especially to Gabriel, the vampire she'd fallen for, the one who still made her heart beat impossibly fast.

Gabriel opened his eyes, capturing her in a fearsome gaze that made her very bones tremble. "But you're *not* normal."

The words stung more than she wanted them to, but he was right. She nodded and lowered her head, unable to look into those green eyes another moment.

But the air shifted around her, and suddenly there he was, standing before her, stealing the breath from her lungs.

Gabriel tucked a finger under her chin, tipping it up until she finally met his eyes.

"You're *extraordinary*," he whispered, the walls lowering for just a moment, just long enough to let her see the wonder in his gaze. The awe.

She opened her mouth to say something in response—anything, just to keep him there, just to keep that look in his eyes. But the walls were already rising again, and before she could utter a word, he released her, turning away and moving to the window, gazing out into the night.

"What happened after?" he asked, absently tracing shapes on the windowpane. It was nearly impossible for her not to remember those same fingers on her skin, tracing slow circles around her nipple, down her stomach, sliding over her clit…

"Jacinda?"

She glanced up to find him watching her, waiting, his gaze as inscrutable as ever.

"What happened after you felt that power inside you?" he asked again.

Blinking away the memories of his searing touch, she said, "It was like my magic just knew what to do. The best way I can describe it is… Okay, remember how I explained to you about spells having different threads?"

"Woven together like a tapestry," he said.

"Exactly. Souls are kind of like that too. It wasn't something I could see, but *feel*—my father's life essence was just one part of his soul. Somehow, I tore it free—magically— and forced it back inside his body. The soul continued on to hell, but my father… He opened his eyes and looked up at me, Gabriel. He sucked in a deep breath, clutched my arm, and came back to me."

"Incredible," he whispered, that same sense of wonder shining in his eyes once more. "But not like a gray? Rotting and mindless?"

"He's not mindless in the way the grays are, driven by instinct and completely devoid of morals and humanity. He's just… I don't know. The best way I can describe it is… blank. He's just blank."

"And physically?"

"His physical body continues to function, but the inactivity is starting to take its toll. Mind, body, and soul are intricately connected—eliminate one, and the others eventually falter. My father is conscious, but unaware. The doctors try to walk and exercise him, but that's getting harder. They tell me his muscles are weakening. Eventually, his organs will fail too."

"Unless you can return his soul," Gabriel said, and she nodded. "Jacinda. Your father... Where is he now?"

"In long-term care at the hospital. Thanks to the compassion of his doctors and nurses—and not a small amount of insurance fraud—his needs are met. They seem to like him too. It's a nice place—I'm just... I'm not sure how much more they can do for him."

"The... hospital?" Gabriel's brow furrowed as he undoubtedly made the connection to the night she'd snuck out of Obsidian. He crossed the room and crouched down before her, reaching for her hands. "Bloody hell, woman. I thought you were sick. Hurt."

"Not me, no."

"You're telling me your father has been in this city the entire time, mere blocks from here?"

She nodded.

"Go to him, then, for fuck's sake!"

A bitter laugh slipped through her lips. "Ah, Prince. If only the offer had come sooner."

"But he's still alive, and—"

"And if Viansa finds out, she'll kill him on sight. For good. Probably in the most brutal way possible. And then his soul will *really* be trapped in hell and there won't be a damned thing I can do about it, necromancy or not."

She pulled out of his grasp and stood up to clear the table, needing something else to focus on besides the abject shittiness of her situation. Besides the new hint of compassion in Gabriel's eyes, where earlier there'd been only revulsion.

It was too much to bear, that simple kindness. Jaci wasn't sure she deserved it. Not yet.

"Anyway," she said, heading into the kitchen with the spent plates and silverware, "tracking down my sister is the priority. I'm not entirely sure what she's even capable of as a fully embodied succubus, but you can bet your ass it's nothing good."

"Right, about that…" Gabriel passed her their empty glasses. "You might want to pour us another round. I've got some news for you, and you can bet your ass it's nothing good."

CHAPTER NINE

"Spontaneous public orgies. So that's a thing now. Who knew?" Jacinda slammed another shot, then removed Gabriel's drink from his hand and downed that one too.

Gabriel sighed. Clearly, the woman was having a hard time processing the videos he'd shown her. After the first clip, she decided to skip the drink mixers and go straight for the hard stuff. Which was fine by him. After everything she'd already told him, the numbing effect of the alcohol was the only thing keeping him even *remotely* calm in the wake of the utter madness.

He no longer wanted to kill her, though. Whether that was a good thing or not remained to be seen.

As if you'd lay a hand on her, Redthorne. Who the bloody hell are you trying to fool?

"Any idea what her end game might be?" he asked, pouring them both another round. "Aside from ruining marriages, mortifying journalists, confounding authorities, and filling the city with naked bodies, that is."

Since the initial dozen or so reports, there hadn't been any more, but that didn't mean it wouldn't happen again. Gabriel knew Viansa wanted to smash the hell gates and turn the city into a demon free-for-all. But stirring up passions throughout the city... Was it just a game? A sideshow to distract them from her true schemes?

Where the fuck *was* she?

"It's not the naked bodies we have to worry about, Prince. It's the dead ones." Jacinda rubbed her eyes and dropped onto the couch, as if the weight of it all had finally caught up to her.

Seeing her like that, soft and vulnerable in her too-big sweatshirt, hair a mess of wild curls piled on top of her head, Gabriel wanted nothing more than to go to her. To take her into his arms, into his bed, and chase away every last one of her nightmares, real or otherwise.

But he still didn't trust her. Didn't *know* her, even— today's confessions were a stark reminder of that.

Where that left him, he had no fucking idea. All Gabriel knew was he didn't want to be far from her. Call it a protective instinct, call it leftover feelings he'd yet to sort out, call it crazy, but it was true.

"Dead ones?" he asked. "As far as I know, none of the... participants... were harmed today. Not physically, anyway."

"Succubi feed on sexual energy," Jacinda said, "the same way vampires feed on blood. Normally, Viansa gets that nourishment by manifesting in dreams—the people she targets are still experiencing a real sexual release, and it sustains her. Now that she's here, she still needs that power source. She got a big boost today, definitely. And it should sustain her for a little while. But—"

"Wait. The people she feeds on are still in danger? Delayed reaction, so to speak?"

"No, nothing like that. If she were targeting just one person repetitively, sure—that would eventually drain them physically. Or just mess with their minds until they broke. This is... something else." She pulled her knees up and tugged the sweatshirt over them. "All that sexual energy will sustain her physical form, but it won't anchor her here in our realm. She's hellbound, and the fact that she's here means she broke the natural order. I don't know exactly how she manifested, but I do know this: in order to stay, she'll need something even stronger than sexual energy to sustain the connection."

"Like what?"

"Death energy. And none of this 'everybody dies, circle of life, isn't it beautiful' bullshit. I'm talking about the dark kind. The horrifying kind."

Gabriel sat beside her on the couch, worry spiking in his chest. "As in..."

He couldn't bring himself to say the words—to drag her back into her memories of the mages last night, the beach— but from the look in her eyes, Gabriel knew she'd understood.

Her words from this morning echoed.

...when you killed them, their emotions—the darkest, worst parts—had nowhere else to go. They filled me right up, fused with my own magic, and turned me into a bomb...

"Unlike me," she said now, "my sister was made to channel that sort of energy. It's the only thing strong enough—and dark enough—to overturn the natural order of hell and bind her here in our realm. And there's really only one way to create it intentionally." She rested her cheek on her knees and closed her eyes. "Ritual human sacrifice."

"*Fuck.* That's the Keepers of the Dark Flame connection, then. She's using them—their rituals—as a power source."

"That's my best, most educated guess."

"We need to find her and destroy her." He rose from the couch, pacing the living room. "How do you kill a bloody succubus? There has to be a way. A spell, a curse, a trap... Something."

"I want her gone more than anyone. Trust me. But we can't kill her, Gabriel. Not yet."

He stopped his pacing and stared at her. "Don't tell me you're going soft over the succubus who tormented you in hell."

"That succubus is the only one who knows exactly where my father's soul is imprisoned. I need answers from her, and I can't get them if she's dead."

"There *has* to be another way to find him."

"If I knew what it was, I'd be all over it." She rose and headed for the balcony doors, staring out across the city just as he'd done. Her breath fogged up the glass, and he watched as she drew a heart, then erased it with her sleeve.

"The only way to save this city—*and* break my family curse, if I recall correctly—is by taking Viansa down. Now you're saying our best play—our *only* play—is off the table?"

"If it means sacrificing my father? Yeah, it's off the table." Jacinda turned to face him, her eyes red and glassy. "I failed him twice, Gabriel. Once when I couldn't destroy the seventh demon in hell. Again when I brought him back from the dead, only to turn him into a walking shell condemned to spend the rest of his pathetic life in the hospital. I will *not* fail him again. Not for you and your family. Not for the entire city. Not for the world. Say whatever you want about me, but that's how I feel."

Gabriel crossed his arms over his chest, again fighting the urge to go to her. "Then you leave me no choice."

She lowered her head and sighed, exhaustion radiating from every part of her. "Do what you think you have to do, Prince. I'm done fighting with you. I've got nothing left for you. So take me down, or get out of my way."

"That's it?" he asked, closing the distance between them. "Take you down or step aside?"

"Unless you've got a miracle up your sleeve."

"Not a miracle, no." He cupped her face, and she raised her eyes to meet his. "Just a witch."

"You know I'll do whatever I can to make this right."

"I know."

"Not just for my dad, but for you. The curse, I mean.

Even if our problems weren't connected, I'd still help you find a way to break it. I still... Gabriel, I..." She closed her eyes, pressing her lips together like she didn't want another word to escape.

"Look at me, Jacinda," he whispered. "Please."

She obeyed, her eyes catching the moonlight, shimmering before him.

Fucking hell, she was beautiful. Captivating.

"Tell me," he whispered.

She reached up and traced the line of his brow, down to his jaw, bringing her hand to rest against his chest. Then, with a sad smile that kicked him right in the gut, she said softly, "You already know."

But he *didn't* know. He was fucking clueless, lost beneath a wave of emotion that threatened to sweep him under, torn between capturing her in another breathless kiss and turning on his heel, bolting out the door, and never looking into those entrancing blue eyes again.

The force of her was almost unnatural, the pull of her, the promise. Despite his best intentions to keep his distance, Gabriel was already leaning close again, heart raging inside him, his gaze locked on her lush, pink mouth...

A knock on the door startled them apart.

"One of your brothers?" Jacinda asked, already heading for the door.

He couldn't tell whether she was relieved or frustrated by the interruption.

Fuck. It was probably Isabelle. He thought he'd have

more time to tell Jacinda about his plan, but the last few hours had passed like minutes, and now it was too late.

"Jacinda, wait. Don't open the door yet."

She turned to look at him over her shoulder, her face pinching with worry. "What's going on?"

He slipped in between Jacinda and the door, barring her from opening it. "Whatever we need to do to track down Viansa—whatever spells, whatever dark magic you need to perform—we both know you can't handle it on your own."

"Wow. Okay. *Wow*." Hurt flashed in her eyes, and she took a step backward, popping her hands on her hips. "I get that you don't trust me—totally fair—but if this is going to work? You need to get over it. I know I fucked up, and I'll *gladly* spend the rest of my life making amends, but not until we nail my sister. We don't have time to—"

"It's not about trust, Jacinda. It's about this being too big for one witch." He stepped close to her again, resting his hands on her shoulders. "You need backup."

"You mean a babysitter?"

"I mean *backup*," he repeated.

"What about you? You said this task binds us. I thought... It's *your* curse! You can't just bail."

There was more to it than his curse, and they both knew it. But Jacinda would no more admit that now than she had earlier.

You already know...

"I'm not bailing," he said. "I'll work every angle I can possibly work, but at the end of the day, I'm not a witch. I can't do magic and craft spells. Can't figure out bindings and hexes and rituals. For that, you need one of your own."

The knock came again.

"Just a moment," Gabriel called out.

Before him, Jacinda shook her head. This time, it wasn't sadness or regret that turned her eyes glassy, but anger, as sharp and hot as he'd ever seen it.

"One of my own," she snapped. "Right. And guess how many of my *own* opened their arms to me when I first arrived here? Guess how many showed even a *hint* of compassion or friendship? I wandered the streets for months. Trying to find a coven, trying to find even a single witch willing to give me a chance. Do you think I would've made myself available to Duchanes if I had another option? If I had friends or witch sisters that could help me get on my feet? They practically spat on me, Gabriel. Like I was a rat. A fucking cockroach."

Gabriel swallowed hard, sadness and anger tightening his throat. To think of her like that, alone after the death of her father, fresh out of a tortured existence in hell…

"From what I understand…" he said, trying to keep his voice even, "the path of a dark witch is often a solitary one. Your own father—"

"It *is* solitary. But that's not always by choice. My father would've loved nothing more than to share his practice with his coven, but they shunned him. They didn't trust him, all because he was more advanced than the elders."

"I understand, but certainly there are witches who don't feel that way. Not all—"

"Seriously? You're about to 'not all witches' me? Trust me, Prince. I've been around enough of them in my time topside to say it with certainty. Yes, all witches. And no, I won't be trusting any of them with this." She stomped into the kitchen in search of the alcohol, but they'd already polished off most of it. "And since when the fuck do *you* trust witches? I thought you hated them. Devil knows you'd never let *me* forget it."

"I don't," he said. "Generally. But there *is* one who's proven to be—"

The door rattled once more. This time, Gabriel opened it. Jacinda wouldn't be swayed by words, anyway.

No sense delaying the inevitable.

He ushered Isabelle inside, keeping one hand firmly on the door, one foot over the threshold, more than eager to make his escape.

"I'm not sure you two were ever properly introduced," he said. "Jacinda Colburn, meet Isabelle Armitage. Bonded Redthorne witch, empath, occasional explorer of the dark arts, and—until we send your sister back to hell in a locked box—your new best mate."

Isabelle nodded sagely, then headed to the table, where she set her magical case and took a seat.

Jacinda merely glared at him, her eyes flashing with warning.

I'm going to kill you, she mouthed.

"I'll check back in a few hours. Oh, and before I forget…" Gabriel grinned, taking more pleasure than he should in Jacinda's obvious irritation. "In the interest of full transparency, Isabelle is also a *damn* good demon exorcist, so *do* try not to piss her off."

With that, he slipped out into the hallway and closed the door behind him, leaving the dark witches to their work, hoping like hell they didn't blow each other up.

CHAPTER TEN

Fuming didn't even *begin* to cover it.

Jaci was ready to explode.

She had nothing against Isabelle specifically—the witch had always been decent to her, if a bit distant.

But Gabriel?

How the hell could he just spring this on her?

Hellfire simmered inside, but she tamped it down, forcing a bright smile.

"Tea?" she asked Isabelle. Her voice was way too high, way too tense.

Not that she could've fooled an empathic witch, anyway. Isabelle would've sensed her feelings the moment she walked into the apartment.

"He didn't tell you he asked me to come, did he?" Isabelle asked.

"Nope." Jaci put the kettle on, then got out two mugs. Honey. Cream. Lemon wedges. The ritual calmed her in ways the crazy-making vampire most certainly did *not*. "Coward," she muttered softly, but of course the elder witch heard.

She probably heard *everything*. Probably had eyes in the back of her head, too.

"Gabriel is no coward," Isabelle said. "But he *is* complicated. All the Redthorne vampires are, of course. But the youngest... He carries a lot of guilt. Shame. He's reckless and impulsive on the best of days, and even when his heart's in the right place, it's not always easy for him to express himself."

Jaci bit back a laugh. Gabriel had no problem *expressing* himself. Shutting the fuck up and listening? That was another story.

But no matter how badly she wanted to throw that vampire right under the bus, she couldn't. Isabelle was absolutely right. Gabriel, for all his faults and issues, *was* complicated. And all the impossibly tangled mess of him stemmed from a world of pain and suffering. She'd figured that much out within three minutes of speaking to him at Bloodbath, long before he told her that gruesome story about his father and his poor pet goat.

And that was just *one* story in an entire lifetime of them.

Augustus Redthorne was a true monster. He and Jaci's mother would probably get along famously. And that, more than anything, softened her heart to Gabriel.

She knew as well as he did what it felt like to be brutalized and rejected by the very people who were supposed to protect you. Supposed to love you. How it broke you inside, turned you into a person who could never fully trust, who held their breath through all the good times, waiting for the bomb to detonate. Waiting for the day everyone in their life turned their backs and walked away.

Or worse.

Once the tea was ready, Jaci assembled everything onto a silver tray, then carried it out to the table where she and Gabriel had shared empanadas and way too many confessions.

Isabelle added a splash of cream to her tea and sipped, her eyebrows lifting in surprise. "Did you create this blend yourself? It's wonderful."

"Yes, thank you. I'm not big on florals in my tea, but I find with the black blends, the vanilla bean balances out the lavender and rose nicely."

"It really does." Isabelle nodded appreciatively, and they enjoyed a few moments of tea and blissful silence. Jaci could almost pretend this was a normal Sunday night—closing out the weekend with a friend, sharing a cup of tea, talking about magic and spellcraft. About anything, really.

But Jaci *wasn't* normal, just like Gabriel had told her. And she never would be.

Finally, the elder witch set down her mug, folded her hands in her lap, and said, "I'm not one for small talk, nor for beating around the bush. May I speak plainly?"

"Please do."

"Gabriel told me what you are, Jacinda. Your origins."

Jaci nodded, grateful for the note of compassion in the woman's tone. "I figured as much."

"I suspected something the night I questioned you at Bloodbath—I sensed a darkness around you, but I couldn't quite put my finger on it. You were actively shielding it from me."

"Not just from you. It's a protective spell I crafted on my first night here. I couldn't—*can't*—let anyone else find out I'm half demon. Vampires, other demons, witches... I wouldn't be safe from any of them."

"No, you wouldn't. Everyone fears that which they do not know and cannot control."

"What about you?" she ventured. "Do you fear me?"

An unexpectedly warm smile spread across Isabelle's face. "No. I know there's much more to you than a hybrid created to ensure the endless dominion of her vile makers."

Jaci returned her smile. "Well, when you put it *that* way..."

"Gabriel also told me about your half-sister, and the other secrets you've kept from him."

Shame heated Jaci's cheeks, but before she could explain herself, Isabelle held up a hand and said, "I'm not here to pass judgment, Jacinda. I haven't the time nor the inclination. You were trying to protect yourself, and Gabriel's actions at Bloodbath didn't exactly lay the groundwork for a relationship built on trust and security."

"Yeah, I wouldn't call those first few weeks a relationship. That was more like a punishment."

Isabelle arched an eyebrow, another smile touching her lips. "*Was?*"

"Things... evolved. We got closer. I wanted to tell him

about everything, but things just got so crazy, and…" She lowered her gaze to the floor, cursing herself inside. "Doesn't matter. If I could rewind the clock and do it over, I would. But I can't."

"The fact that you want to, though… That's growth."

"Really? Feels like one step forward, a hundred steps backward to me. At the rate I'm screwing things up lately, I'll be back in diapers before you know it."

"Growth is rarely a straight line, especially where love is concerned. There are—"

"*Love*?" Jaci forced out a laugh, ignoring the wave of heat the word unleashed in her chest. "Have you *met* Gabriel Redthorne? That man is utterly incapable of emotion, let alone forming an actual relationship with another person."

Isabelle said nothing. Just nodded her head and smiled like a wise woman of old, making Jaci hot and itchy and more than ready to jump on a different train. *Any* train.

"So," Jaci said brightly. "As much as I love a good tea party, I'm pretty sure that's not why you're here."

"I'm *always* available for a tea party," Isabelle said, "but you're right. I'm here because I want to help with this Viansa situation."

"Just like that?"

"Just like that."

"You do realize Viansa is a dangerous succubus, an original demon with the powers of mind control and illusion magic, and—not to put too fine a point on it—a psychotic bitch?"

"All the more reason I want to help. The vampire family I'm bonded to—a relationship I cherish more than you could possibly know—is in grave danger. That alone is cause for my involvement. But one of those vampires is also *very* worried about you—whether he'll admit it out loud or not—and I can't blame him. This is big, Jacinda. Bigger than you. He knows you need help—more than he can give you on his own."

The thought of Gabriel's concern prickled her insides. It felt too heavy, just like his compassion had earlier. A thing she didn't deserve and didn't even know how to carry.

"Viansa is *my* sister," she said defensively. "*My* disaster to fix."

Again, Isabelle said nothing. Just lifted the mug to her lips, sipping her tea as if she had all the time in the world for Jaci to come to her senses.

After an agonizingly long moment of silence, Isabelle finally said, "Accepting help is not a sign of weakness. Quite the opposite, actually. It takes a strong woman to recognize when she needs it, and an even stronger one to take it when it's offered."

The words cut right to the heart of the matter, leaving Jaci completely raw and exposed. Her gaze darted around the living room, desperate for something else to land on, for a subject change, for an excuse to show Isabelle the exit, run to the bedroom, and burrow deep beneath her blankets, hiding away from the world.

But in the end, there *was* nothing else to land on. All Jaci had left was the truth.

"I'm sorry," she said softly. "It's just… Where I come from, help isn't offered without strings, and blindly accepting it is the fastest way to eternal damnation."

Isabelle nodded, her eyes reflecting a deep understanding Jaci hadn't even realized she'd needed. "You're not in hell anymore, sweetness. Try to remember that."

A tear slipped down Jaci's cheek, but Isabelle's soft touch on her hand brought a new smile to her face.

"Okay," Jaci whispered. "I think I can manage that."

"Good." Isabelle released her hand and reached for her case, retrieving a battered grimoire and three occult textbooks so old the spines had split, held together now with nothing more than string and a prayer. "Shall we begin?"

CHAPTER ELEVEN

"I have a dear friend at NYU—professor of occult studies," Isabelle explained. "She's a witch, and the smartest woman I know when it comes to demonic lore. These texts are on loan from her private collection."

"This is amazing." Jaci flipped through one of them, the pages as thin as onion skin, each one crowded with illustrations and theories, symbols, rituals for summoning and banishing, stories older than time. "I was born and raised in hell, and *I* didn't even know half this stuff."

"Demons are ancient beings," Isabelle said. "You were in hell for a blink by comparison—it's not surprising that much of this would be unfamiliar to you. A lot of it is conjecture, mind you, but there's a grain of truth in everything. My hope is that if we put our heads together—and our magical know-how—we can find the grain of truth that will help us bind Viansa's powers *and* help your father."

The mention of her father sent a pang through Jaci's heart. "Gabriel told you about that too?"

"He did." Isabelle sighed. "My father has Alzheimer's. Sometimes it feels like I'm watching him disappear before my very eyes. I understand what it's like to lose a beloved parent, and if there's even a chance I can spare someone else that pain…"

A knot of emotion tightened Jaci's throat. "Thank you, Isabelle."

Jaci had just put the kettle on for another cup of tea when the vampire prince returned, entering the apartment as he always did—uninvited, unannounced, wrapped in the evergreens-in-winter scent that drove her wild and sucked all the air out of the room.

"I've been thinking," he proclaimed suddenly, confidently, as if the women should both bow at his feet.

"Have you, now?" Jaci pressed her hand to her chest, her eyes wide with mock concern. "Are you all right, Prince? Maybe you'd better sit down. Shall I fetch a cold compress?"

Isabelle snickered. "And on that note, I think I'll leave you two to catch up."

"No!" Jaci practically shouted. "I mean… You haven't had your second cup yet. And the lore books were just getting good."

"I'll leave them for you. And I'll take a raincheck on the tea." With a covert wink, Isabelle grabbed her coat and the rest of her things, leaving only the books behind. "I'll be back tomorrow morning, Jacinda. Remember what I said."

Jaci nodded and thanked the woman, but the idea of being alone with Gabriel again left her completely off-kilter.

Growth is rarely a straight line, especially where love is concerned…

One of those vampires is also very worried about you…

Of all the things Isabelle had said tonight, the parts about Gabriel clamored loudest in her mind.

"Looks like you two got on well," Gabriel said, a hint of smugness in his tone.

"Isabelle's a formidable woman," she replied. "And kind. I actually like her, if you can believe that."

"She has that effect. Wears you down with all that wisdom and authenticity."

Jaci smiled. "I can see why you trust her. And maybe…"

"And maybe what?" Gabriel closed the distance between them, crowding her against the kitchen counter-top, peering down at her with those devilish eyes.

"Maybe I *could* use the help," she admitted. "A little bit."

"Hmm." Gabriel leaned closer, resting his hands on the countertop behind her, caging her inside his arms. "Is this the part where you admit I was right about something?"

"You made *one* helpful suggestion, Prince," she teased. "Don't go getting a big head over it."

"Still. I was right. That's something."

The air crackled between them, their mouths hovering in dangerously-close-enough-to-kiss territory, the heat of his body radiating against her as she struggled to maintain control.

"Admit it," he said, a dare flashing in his eyes, a smirk twisting his sexy mouth, "and I'll set you free."

What if I don't want *you to set me free?*

The thought bounced around in her head, stupid and annoying and absolutely *not* getting a say in this.

"Gabriel," she said firmly, torn between giving in and pushing him away, wishing like hell things weren't so damn confusing between them now.

"Yes?" he whispered, his breath warm on her lips. "You were saying? Something about me being right, I believe?"

Could they just go back to hating each other and occasionally fucking? Did it have to mean anything more than that? Did she have to crave his stupid smile and his sexy bare feet and the way she sometimes caught him staring at her, even when he was trying to act like he hadn't been paying attention?

"Gabriel," she said again, pressing a hand to his chest. "Maybe it's best if we just—"

The teakettle whistled, piercing the air and shattering the supercharged moment.

"Tea!" she blurted out. "Best if we have tea." Taking advantage of his momentary distraction, she ducked out from under his arms and headed for the stove, never more grateful for the wonder of boiling water.

By the time the tea had steeped, the flirty moment had passed, both of them retreating to their separate emotional corners. The only thing she knew for sure was that neither of them had any clue how to navigate this strange territory. For all the distrust and anger still simmering between them, it was clear their attraction to each other hadn't dimmed a bit.

But was that all it was? Intense attraction, heightened by the fact that they'd started out as enemies? That she'd blown whatever trust and friendship they might've built to bits?

Had there even *been* anything to blow up—anything other than wild, mutual lust? Or had she imagined the glimpses of longing and vulnerability in his otherwise icy eyes?

And why the hell—after everything that'd happened between them, after everything he'd made clear this morning about where they stood—was her heart still drumming out a rapid-fire beat, all for him?

Gabriel doesn't do feelings, she reminded herself. *Especially not for the witch-demon who betrayed him.*

Jaci needed to remember that. The past, however recent, no longer mattered. Love, lust, temporary insanity… The label wasn't important, because whatever it was had vanished the moment she confessed her secrets.

There was no going back. Only forward, no matter how many stumbles and steps it took.

Back in the living room, they took seats on opposite ends—Gabriel on the couch, Jaci at the table. She told him about Isabelle's books, about the research they'd planned to do together. He asked a few questions about the lore, and then, out of nowhere, "Your original plan… You said you needed my heart to bind Viansa's powers. How would that work?"

SARAH PIPER

The question caught her completely off guard. She faltered, nearly dropping her tea. "Gabriel, I'm not... I wasn't going to. I—"

"Answer the question, Jacinda."

Tightening her grip on the mug, she sighed and said, "Viansa is the demon who bound your curse—the dark power that ensures both its potency and its permanence. The curse runs through your blood, through your very heart, and it's deeply connected to her magic—like, on a cellular level."

"Okay. But I'm not quite following how the binding spell would work."

"Are you familiar with the ancient Egyptian pantheon?"

"Somewhat."

"The goddess Serket was associated with scorpions and other venomous creatures. The ancients believed she caused their stings, so they also called upon her in spells and rituals to heal or protect against them. Two sides of the same magical coin, so to speak." Jaci sipped her tea. "Essentially, a connection forged by a certain magic can also be broken by that same magic when that magic is intentionally altered for a different purpose."

"Fight like with like," he said.

"Something like that, yes."

"But why the heart, specifically? Why not my blood? Or a finger, for that matter? Something that wouldn't require me to be turned into a gray."

"Our hearts hold our very essences, Gabriel. Not only do they control the flow of blood throughout every part of

104

our bodies, but they record the moments of our lives, beat by beat, until the moment of our death. The Egyptians knew this too. It's why they mummified the heart but discarded the brain, thinking it a useless organ." Jaci shook her head, shame burning through her chest. "That day, when I finally translated the message from the Tarot, it all just clicked. I realized the heart was the most powerful part of your being—powerful enough to bind an ancient demon's powers."

"The Tarot?" he asked with a dark chuckle. "So a deck of cards told you to kill me?"

She looked up and met his eyes, but there was no malice there. If anything, her explanations only seemed to further intrigue him.

"Not exactly," she said. "It's… it's better if I show you."

CHAPTER TWELVE

Jaci retrieved the carved wooden box that held her cards, tucked between two rosemary plants on the kitchen windowsill.

Returning to the living room and sitting next to Gabriel on the couch, she rifled through the cards until she found the three from the reading the other night, then laid them out on the coffee table:

Three of Knives, with the silver-haired girl sitting in the snow in the middle of a cemetery, clutching a dagger before a white rose dripping with blood.

Death, the pale corpse wrapped in a black serpent, waiting to rise again.

And last, the Ten of Knives, the ultimate betrayal, a woman stabbed with a dagger, bleeding out on white bedding embroidered with black roses.

She did her best to explain their meanings, the feelings she got from each one that night, the ultimate message she'd interpreted. "It's hard to describe, but after sitting with it for a bit, I just knew. Everything clicked into place. The missing ingredient for the binding spell was the heart of the cursed vampire himself."

Gabriel picked up the Death card, examining it closely— almost reverently. "And that bit about turning me into a gray?"

"It would've been the only way to keep the heart intact," she admitted, doing her best to keep her voice even. "If you actually died, you'd turn to ash and so would your heart."

He dropped the card as if it'd suddenly burned him. "Tricky business, carving up a vampire."

In the awkward silence that followed, Jaci reassembled the cards, then began shuffling them absently, calmed by the motion, by the familiar feel of the cards against her palm. Even now, when she hadn't intended on doing an actual reading, she felt their magic—a tingling warmth in her hands, a buzz that ran up her arms and straight into her heart.

Gabriel shifted on the couch, his thigh brushing against hers, and one of the cards jumped suddenly from the deck.

It landed face-up on the coffee table, showing them a pale woman lying on a bed of white roses, blood leaking from her lips, a single red rose draped over her shoulder. A death's-head hawkmoth perched on her arm as her vampire lover lay beside her, nuzzling her neck.

"The Lovers card?" Gabriel quirked an eyebrow and

picked it up, his eyes sparkling with mischief. "And what does *this* one mean, I wonder?"

Jaci's heart skipped a beat as she rushed to explain. "It's… complicated. Like any card, sometimes it can be taken literally—lovers, a relationship, intense desire, a deeply intimate bond, sex. Other times it's more figurative. It may signify a crossroads or a choice."

"Two sides of the magical coin?" he asked, echoing her earlier words. "So you believe love is a choice?"

"I… wait. What? No, I didn't say the *choice* was about love. It's a metaphor. You *do* know what a metaphor is, right, Prince?"

"You *do* know how to answer a question, right, witch?" he teased.

"Did you ask one?"

"I asked," he said, turning to face her fully, that maddening smirk playing at his lips, "if you believe love is a choice. Do you?"

"I… I think…" Jaci's heart thudded, mouth going dry, every part of her body supremely aware of his gaze. It swept down her face, down her chest, right down to her hands fisted tight against each thigh. "I think you still owe *me* an answer, Prince. You never told me about your so-called epiphany."

He laughed—his rare, real laugh—rich and warm and buttery, a sound that made her heart gallop even harder. "Nice save, witch. Truly."

"So? What's the story?"

His laughter faded, and for a minute she regretted

asking for his thoughts. But sitting around making innu-endos over sexy Tarot cards wasn't going to help them find her sister, and it certainly wasn't going to fix the colossal mess she'd made of things between them.

"In everything you've told me," he said, "I keep coming back to this: the magical connection to Viansa is based on the curse, not on me specifically."

"Right."

"So for the purposes of a binding spell, *any* of my broth-ers' hearts would work equally well, yes?"

She ran her hands down her spandex-covered thighs. "I mean, sure. Technically any of the Redthorne hearts would've done it. Same with Charley's, assuming Dorian's the one who sired her. It's all the same sire line—which means it's the same curse. The same direct connection to Viansa."

"That, Jacinda Colburn, is the best news you've given me all night." He grinned at her, very close to unleashing another laugh.

"Don't tell me to sacrifice one of your brothers, Gabriel. No way. I don't care which one of them pissed in your Lucky Charms this morning, it's *not* happening."

"Shooting me down already," he teased. "Shame on you, Jacinda. You haven't even allowed me to finish."

Still holding the Lovers card, he leaned back on the couch, one arm bent behind his head, legs parted, his muscled form on exquisite, drool-worthy display. It would be so, so easy for her to crawl into his lap, lean in and kiss the spot behind his earlobe, slide her hand down the front of those jeans and—

"Do you know how your former master became a vampire?" he asked, snapping her right out of her fantasy.

"Oh, sure," she said, rolling her eyes. "The asshole could never shut up about it. Some noble vampire lord in Paris saw his untapped potential and plucked him from the slums, bestowing upon him the gift of immortality, yadda yadda yadda."

"I don't know about untapped potential, but I do know about the noble lord. King, more accurately. It was my father, Jacinda. Augustus Redthorne."

Jaci gasped. "Renault was sired by your father?"

Gabriel nodded and lowered his gaze, his cool demeanor cracking just a fraction. "Before... before my brother Malcolm died, he told us he'd met with Duchanes and all but confirmed it. Duchanes was already showing symptoms. He's the one who told us about the curse—he must've learned about it from Chernikov."

"Holy shit, Gabriel." Jaci closed her eyes, memories flashing through her mind. It all made perfect sense in retrospect; she'd seen it herself—Renault's growing avoidance of the sunlight, his constant need to feed, the physical exhaustion he tried to hide at all costs, requiring her magical intervention more and more often. Absent a logical explanation, she'd attributed it to his frustrations with the Redthornes and his endless scheming to overthrow Dorian. She had no idea he was afflicted by dark magic.

She opened her eyes, meeting his gaze. "If this is true—"

"It is. I don't know why it didn't occur to me earlier. When you confessed your plans for the binding spell this morning, I couldn't... I saw red. Bloody red. That's all there was for me. After that, I was so focused on hating..." He trailed off and lowered his gaze, but Jaci knew what he'd meant to say.

"Hating me," she whispered.

Gabriel nodded. "I was angry, Jacinda. I'm *still* angry. I just... I'm trying to understand you. To understand all of this. I've never felt so... But then I met you and everything changed so fast, and it was... And I..." He trailed off again, and this time she didn't fill in the gaps.

She didn't have the courage to ask what he felt, what meeting her had changed, what words were supposed to come after that "I."

So instead, she squared her shoulders and said, "We have to find the Keepers of the Dark Flame. We already know they're connected to Duchanes. They'll know how to find him."

"Perhaps."

"I can go in undercover. I know what to expect this time. I—"

"No." He looked up again, his eyes suddenly blazing. "Absolutely not. You went in undercover last time and look how that turned out."

"But this time the demon won't be warning them in advance. It won't be a setup."

"I don't care. You're not going anywhere *near* those mages, Jacinda."

"But what if that's our best shot?"

"Then we'll take our second-best. Cole's still investigating Duchanes' real estate purchases in New Jersey. Unless that lead turns out to be a dead end, we're not making a move—especially not one that involves you risking your life with the Dark Flame mages. One hundred percent out of the question. Understood?"

With a deep sigh, Jaci nodded. "Let's just hope Cole finds something."

"That wolf won't quit until he's sniffed out every last shred of evidence. So when he finds Duchanes—*when*, not if —then we'll figure out how to capture him, pseudo-kill him, resurrect him, and let you do your hocus-pocus." Gabriel shook his head, blowing out a breath. "Oh, and that's assuming we find your sister too, and get them in the same location long enough to execute the plan, all without getting ourselves killed in the process."

"Is that all?" she teased.

Gabriel shrugged. "No small feat, Jace."

Jace. She didn't know whether to feel more hopeful about the sweetly casual use of her name or the news about Duchanes and the curse, but either way, things were already looking up, and she couldn't help the new smile stretching across her face.

"If there's one thing you've always known about me, Prince," she said, "it's that I *live* for a challenge."

Gabriel glanced at the Lovers card still in his hand, then back to her. "That's precisely what I'm afraid of, little moonflower."

CHAPTER THIRTEEN

"Zachary Colburn is receiving excellent care," Colin said, sliding a folder across Gabriel's desk. "It's a small hospital, but his doctors and nurses are among the best in the country. They're tending to his every need. From what I could determine from my examination, he's as healthy as can be expected, given the circumstances."

Flipping through Colin's notes, Gabriel leaned back in his chair and sighed, marginally satisfied with the report. "Best news we could hope for, I suppose."

It was the day after he'd learned about Jacinda's father —about all of her secrets, really—and today, he was back in his office at Obsidian, Jacinda tending bar down on the main level, both of them determined to put some normalcy back into their lives. It may not last long—Viansa had gone off the radar, almost certainly plotting another dramatic play—but at this point, even a few hours of peace was a welcome respite.

"And the bills?" Gabriel asked.

"The balance has been paid in full," Colin replied. "Dr. Daniels confirmed all future bills will be automatically deducted from the anonymous account you set up."

"Did she ask questions about your involvement?"

"I pre-empted them with a bit of compulsion and a sizable donation."

Gabriel opened his eyes and nodded. He figured it would come to that. "Thanks for handling it."

Colin turned pensive, his eyes getting that glazed look they sometimes got when he was having a good think.

"What is it?" Gabriel asked.

"I don't like the idea of leaving him there," Colin said, as if he'd suddenly decided Zachary was his patient to care for.

Colin was like that, though. Somehow he'd inherited all of their father's scientific curiosity and none of the bastard's cruelty, driven instead by their mother's kindness, compassion, and a deep sense of rightness Gabriel couldn't even come close to understanding.

Of all his brothers, it was Colin he'd missed most during their fifty-year estrangement. Only now, with the benefit of hindsight, did he see how much time he wasted in Las Vegas, his only companions his own bitterness and resentment. Even for a family of immortals, life was never a guarantee.

Losing Malcolm had taught him that.

Never again, Gabriel vowed. No matter how terrible things got, no matter how many threats and insults they hurled, no matter how much blood they spilled from one another's veins, Gabriel would never turn his back on his brothers again.

"It's a human hospital, Gabriel." Colin leaned forward in his chair, tapping a finger against the folder on the desk. "And they're caring for the needs of his human body. But Zachary's issues are fundamentally supernatural—something his doctors are completely unaware of. They only know how to treat his physical condition, which is steadily deteriorating. How long until they no longer know what to do with him? Dr. Daniel's already mentioned they're mostly just trying to keep him comfortable."

Gabriel winced. "Sounds like the kiss of death."

"I want him transferred for private care."

"Provided by whom?"

He didn't answer. Didn't have to.

"Colin, what of your pediatrics practice? You've only just hung out your shingle."

"I can manage both." Colin smiled, spreading his hands before him. "From birth to advanced aging, mortal or immortal, human or supernatural, Dr. Colin Redthorne provides a full spectrum of medical care."

"Already got the advertisement scripted, I see." Gabriel grinned, but it didn't last. Tucking the folder into the desk drawer, he said, "Unfortunately, Zachary can't be moved. At least not yet, and certainly not by anyone connected to House Redthorne or to Jacinda. I don't even want her to know about your visit—it'll only worry her."

"Why?"

"She's concerned about discovery, and with good reason. If Viansa learns Zachary is still alive, she'll end him. Brutally and permanently."

"If he can't be moved, then I'll appoint myself as an outside consultant in his care. I'll tend to him at the hospital alongside his current team, using minimal compulsion only when absolutely necessary to avoid arousing suspicion, and—"

"Colin, I appreciate your concern for the man, but we can't risk it. Viansa knows about the royal family—knows we're connected to Jacinda. Today's visit was a necessary risk to assess the situation and secure his care going forward. But you can't see him again—can't even contact his doctors for an update. Not until we deal with Viansa. Understood?"

"Of course. Worth a try, though, right? I was thinking I… I mean, it… The situation is… I…" Confusion clouded Colin's eyes, and he blinked rapidly, his face turning ghostly pale.

"Colin? Are you all right?"

"I… I'm sorry, brother." He scrubbed a hand over his face. "Do you have any blood? I'm suddenly quite famished."

Gabriel retrieved two glass bottles from the small refrigerator he kept stocked in the office bar. "Would you like it mixed with anything?"

"Undiluted is probably best."

Gabriel opened the bottles and passed one to his brother, then reclaimed his seat behind the desk, watching as Colin downed the entire thing in seconds.

"Do you need more?" Gabriel asked, offering him the second bottle.

"No, thank you." Colin forced a smile, but Gabriel wasn't buying it.

"Colin, are you—"

"It's nothing. I'm just a bit tired."

"You don't get tired. And I've seen you get so involved in your work you forget to feed for days at a time, but it's never left you so... so out of sorts."

Colin waved away the concern. "Between setting up the practice, tending to my patients, and the ongoing work with Father's research—"

"Father's research?" Gabriel took a swig of the blood, feeling like he needed the boost. Talk of their father always wore him thin. "Still barking up that tree, then?"

"Say what you will about Father, but this is important work. The cure for vampirism needs heavy modification if it's ever to become a viable option. Right now, it's simply too dangerous to leave in its current iteration."

A now-familiar ache settled into Gabriel's chest. He knew all too well the dangers of their father's so-called cure. In its current formulation, it turned a vampire into a human, effectively "curing" him. The side effects were another matter; the moment the body returned to its human state, it aged to its present human age—rapidly. Not even a formerly immortal vampire could outrun the curse of time.

That cure had killed his father. And it'd destroyed

Malcolm's body as well, allowing Dorian to defeat the demon possessing it—Azerius.

Malcolm, of course, had not survived.

Gabriel took another long pull from the bottle.

"I suppose I've just been burning the candle at both ends," Colin said, but Gabriel wasn't convinced.

All the explanations and excuses in the world couldn't paint over the truth, and the frightened look in Colin's eyes —there and gone in a blink—confirmed it.

The curse.

It was starting to affect Colin.

Gabriel knew all too well the signs. Weakening muscles. Loss of coordination. Sensitivity to sunlight. Inability to absorb the nutrients they needed from blood. The haze that sometimes blew through the mind like a thick fog.

Dorian had been the first to feel it. Then Gabriel. Now Colin. He imagined Charlotte wasn't too far behind.

Aiden was the question mark. Since he was neither a Redthorne by blood nor sired by one, his fate came down to the precise wording of the curse, which none of them knew.

"We'll find Viansa," Gabriel said firmly, "and break this bloody curse. I promise you."

"I know. But I'm fine—really. As I said, I just need—"

A knock on the door saved them both from faking their way through more of Colin's flimsy explanations.

"Come in," Gabriel said.

The door swung open, revealing Cole in his usual flannel and jeans, cigarette growing out of his mouth. Behind him, Jacinda dazzled in black leather pants and a silver sequined top, hair wild and loose, cascading over her shoulders.

After last night, he could scarcely meet her eyes without seeing that Tarot card—the Lovers. Without hearing her soft voice whispering through his mind.

Like any card, sometimes it can be taken literally—lovers, a relationship, intense desire, a deeply intimate bond, sex…

"Got some news for ya, Little Red," Cole said, exhaling a plume of smoke. "The good, the bad, *and* the ugly."

CHAPTER FOURTEEN

"Intel panned out." Leaning back against the wall, Cole lifted a foot and smashed his cigarette butt into the sole of his boot, then swapped it for a fresh one from his pack. He lit it and took a deep drag. "That's the good news. Duchanes recently bought two properties in Newark—a big ol' warehouse and a brownstone not far from it, both in his own name. I did some drive-bys on the locations, snooped around as best I could. Didn't want to get too close without backup."

"What did you see?"

"Nothing much going on at the brownstone. Looks like he lives there, maybe uses it to house his favorite blood slaves. Doesn't spend much time there, though. All the action's over at the warehouse, which is where the bad news comes in."

"How so?"

"No windows, lots of beefed-up security. Makes it a

bitch to suss out what's really going on inside those walls. And here comes the ugly—Duchanes is planning something big. Fuck of a lot bigger than the shit we busted up here at Bloodbath."

He described the exterior warehouse scene: rogue demons and a ragtag group of heavily armed panther shifters serving as guard dogs, with everyone else coming and going at all hours, a constant stream of supernaturals—demons, vampires from Duchanes' own house and others remaining loyal after the Bloodbath massacre, and—confirming Gabriel's worst suspicions—mages.

"Keepers of the Dark Flame?" Jacinda asked. Gabriel heard the change in her pulse, scented a hint of fear in her blood. She was still standing near the door next to Cole, and now he rose from his chair, gesturing for her to take it. When she did, he put one hand on her shoulder and squeezed.

It was all the touch he dared to offer. Anything more would've driven him over the edge, and he'd have her spread out on the desk in a bloody heartbeat, that silver top torn away like gift wrapping as he licked and sucked and—

"No tellin'," Cole said. "All I know is there was a lot of 'em, and they were packin' some serious mojo. The kind that makes the hairs on your neck stand up, even from all the way across the street."

"How many?" Gabriel asked.

"Mages? Between what I saw and what I could scent, a hundred at least. Far as the rest, we're lookin' at a few dozen demons and bloodsuckers, no other shifters other than the ten or so working security, and…" He sucked in another deep drag from the cigarette, then shook his head in disgust. "Grays. I can smell those fuckers two states over, and that place is *full* of 'em. The concentration of their scents stayed pretty consistent, though, which tells me they're not moving. I didn't see any come in or out—they stayed behind the walls."

"In cages," Jacinda said with a shudder. "He captures some, breeds the rest, and keeps them all locked up until he needs them. He likes to release them in groups at strategic locations."

"We've seen it in action," Gabriel said. "More than once. What I don't understand is—if he's got this army amassed, why not just unleash it? Grays may not be the most cunning foe, but in a swarm, they could easily overwhelm an opponent. Hell, he could set them loose inside Obsidian, and by the time we realized what was happening, half the supernaturals here would be piles of ash."

Colin, who'd remained silent throughout the exchange, rose from the chair and headed for the stash of blood, helping himself to another bottle. "Are you sure you shouldn't close Obsidian," he asked, turning to face them. "At least until we've taken down this army?"

Jacinda let out a heavy sigh. "Those grays aren't the army, guys. Just the test subjects."

"Test subjects?" Colin asked.

"Renault won't release them en masse until he's perfected the resurrection spells—the initial amulets were just a prototype. Not only that, but I'm sure he's working on other magical enhancements too."

"That could explain the heavy mage presence," Cole said.

Jacinda nodded. "He was constantly contracting with new witches and mages to make different spells and charms. Keeping the grays from turning to ash was just the first step—Renault wants a *true* army. One that can outsmart, outrun, and outfight any supernatural enemy he sets his sights on. Now that he's hooked up with the Keepers of the Dark Flame? There's no telling what they're planning, only that it's going to suck. And let's not forget the Viansa connection," she said, as if any of them could.

"Forgive me for being a little slow on the uptake," Cole said, "but who the fuck's Viansa?"

Gabriel sighed. He'd forgotten Cole was out of the loop on that particular story.

Skipping over the bit about Jacinda's lies—and the fact that Viansa was a blood relative—he did his best to give Cole the overview: evil succubus terrorizing the city, plotting to unleash hell on earth, fueled with help from the dark mages, well versed in mind control, strong penchant for orgies, et cetera, et cetera.

"I always miss the good shit." Cole laughed. "And you Redthornes can't help but step *right* in it, every damn time. Hell, wherever there's a steaming pile, a Redthorne boot is sure to follow."

"Not intentionally," Gabriel said. "Anyway, as you can see, we're fighting battles on multiple fronts, and those fronts all seem to be converging on three key players: Viansa, Duchanes, and these Keepers of the Dark Flame. My hope is that taking one down will weaken the whole lot, but we can't know that for sure. Viansa is the most powerful, and therefore the biggest immediate threat, but it's likely she needs the mages' help to remain in our realm, so taking them out could work just as well as hitting her directly. Duchanes' connection is a bit more nebulous. Partnering with a succubus is a dangerous play, even for him."

"I imagine he wants what he's always wanted," Colin said. "To eliminate the royal family and take his place as vampire king."

"We need to wipe out the whole damn operation," Cole said, slicing his hand through the air. "One fell swoop."

"I'm with you," Gabriel said, "but we can't allow it to be another Bloodbath. We charged in hot and heavy that night —no plan, no solid intel—because Sasha's life was at stake. We did the right thing—no question—but we lost Duchanes, and now he's rebuilding from a position of strength. We can't risk that happening again. There are too many disgruntled supernaturals looking for the promise of something better—a promise Duchanes is all too eager to make."

"Plenty of folks don't like that your brother's cozy with Rogozin," Cole said. "Especially the bloodsuckers. They think Duchanes would do a better job regulating the factions without selling out to the so-called enemy."

"Never mind the fact that Duchanes is working with his own demons—some of them likely on the Rogozin payroll as well." Gabriel clenched his jaw, wishing they'd taken out Duchanes the night of the fundraiser, long before the rest of this shit spiraled so out of control.

"Desperate, angry people are easy to manipulate," Colin said. "We've seen it throughout history. And Duchanes is nothing if not a master manipulator."

"All the more reason we need to do this right," Gabriel said. "I won't risk him catching wind of this and vanishing on us again. We need a *lot* more intel and an ironclad plan. Only then do we make our move."

"And in the meantime?" Jacinda asked. "We can't just pretend everything's normal. Viansa could be anywhere, gearing up to drop another bomb."

"Finding Viansa is our top priority," he said, squeezing her shoulder again. "You and Isabelle need to keep working the magical and research angles, and I'll keep working mine. I've cast a wide net—I've got associates and royal guards out all over the city looking for her. I've also increased security at Obsidian as well as at our apartment building, inside and out."

Jacinda nodded, her shoulders relaxing beneath his touch.

"For now," Gabriel said to the group, "we play it cool and keep moving forward. From what you've said, Cole, it doesn't sound like Duchanes is ready to make his next move just yet. We may have a little time there."

"Agreed," Cole replied, "but I wouldn't bet on much. Hate for us to get caught with our dicks in the wind on this one."

"No fucking way," Gabriel said.

"Someone needs to tell Dorian and Aiden," Colin said. "They'll want to know what's going on."

"I'm headin' back upstate tonight." Cole took another drag, his lungs crackling right along with the cigarette. "I'll drop by Ravenswood and fill everyone in."

"Thank you," Gabriel said. "But I want you to make it clear to Dorian we're handling it. We'll keep him in the loop, but he's got too many other things to focus on right now—he doesn't need to micromanage this."

"I'll do my best," Cole said, "but I think we both know your brother will be up your ass like a cheap G-string by sunrise."

"Cheap G-strings are the *worst*!" Jacinda cracked up.

"My *brother*," Gabriel said, trying hard not to be jealous at how easily the wolf had made her laugh, "needs to learn the fine art of delegating."

"Yeah, good luck with that," Cole said. "In the meantime, what about Duchanes? We probably shouldn't leave that warehouse unattended for too long."

"No, you're right," Gabriel said. "Think you can do a little more recon without getting yourself into trouble?"

"Not a chance, Little Red." Cole laughed, blowing out a final plume of gray smoke. "But when has this wolf *ever* said no to trouble?"

CHAPTER FIFTEEN

"Sapphire and tonic," the woman at the end of the bar called out, "and a word with the head bartender, if she can spare a minute."

Her tone was sharp and severe, sending goosebumps across Jaci's arms.

She made the drink in record time, then turned to face her customer, her stomach twisting. Cole and Colin had just left, Gabriel was checking in with his security guys, and Maritza was busy helping the cocktail servers at the other end of the bar.

If shit went south, Jaci was on her own.

"Charley," she said cautiously, handing over the drink. "Good to see you again. Love the jacket."

It wasn't a lie—the dark-green velvet looked amazing with her auburn hair—but Charley clearly wasn't in the mood for compliments.

She sat on the barstool, sucked down the entire drink in

one fell swoop, then slammed the glass onto the bar, a murderous rage glinting in her eyes. "I warned you not to hurt him, Jaci. I fucking warned you."

"Great." Jaci let out a deep sigh. "I take it Dorian gave you the scoop?"

"Scoop? *Scoop*?" Charley glanced around the bar to make sure no one was listening too closely, then leaned in, dropping her voice to a harsh whisper. "You're a fucking demon. Your evil, curse-binding sister is out there sexing up the whole city. Dark mages want you dead. You lied to Gabriel about *all* of it, putting him right smack in the middle of your fucked-up family drama—drama that could get him killed. And you call that a *scoop*?"

Jaci made Charley a fresh drink, then set the glass down hard in front of her, refusing to be cowed. "*Half* demon, vampire queen. If you're picking this fight, you'd better know who you're up against."

Jaci let her eyes turn demon-black, just for a second. She wanted to send a spark of hellfire into Charley's lungs—just a few embers to put her in her place—but thought better of harming the vampire king's future bride.

Plus, Charley had a point. She *had* warned Jaci, and Jaci fucked it all up.

"Don't you give me those black eyes!" Charley shout-whispered. "I should tear your throat out for that."

"Are we taking this outside, bloodsucker? Or are you going to tear my throat out in front of all these customers?"

"Outside *was* the plan." Charley took another healthy swig of the drink, the rage in her eyes lowering from a boil to a simmer. A soft curse escaped, quickly turning into a snicker. "The thing is, Jaci, I really fucking like you."

Jaci's chest flared with an unfamiliar warmth. She liked Charley too. In another life, she imagined they'd probably be pretty good friends.

She let her eyes return to their usual blue, the hellfire cooling inside.

"Also," Charley continued, "my future brother-in-law would stake me if I laid a finger on you—even a finger laid in his defense—which would make Christmas dinner *super* awkward. I mean, the Redthornes just started talking again after half a damn century. The last thing they need is a catfight tearing them apart for another fifty years. I swear, those royal vampire man-babies can hold a grudge like—"

"Charley? As much as I appreciate the deep dive on the Redthorne family history, I'd rather skip the pregame and get right to the beat-down. Anticipating my own demise gives me anxiety."

"Tempting offer, but…" Charley let out a resigned groan, the very last of her anger melting away. "I think you need a friend more than you need a beat-down. And that's saying something, because you need a beat-down something *fierce*."

"A friend." Jaci practically snorted. "Right. And you're volunteering? Thirty seconds ago, you were ready to slaughter me."

Charley lifted a shoulder and sipped her drink, peering at Jaci over the rim of her glass.

That Charley didn't trust her was obvious. So why the

hell was she sitting here, dangling the f-word out in front of her like a bone for an attention-starved dog?

Jaci waited another beat for Charley to answer, but her response never came.

"I've lived my entire life without friends," Jaci said, ignoring the burn of guilt and fear when she thought of Meech, who still hadn't answered a summoning. "Pretty sure I'll survive for another…. well, however many days I've got left."

"Is that what you want? To *survive*?"

"You say it like it's a bad thing."

"It's not bad. I just think you should aim a little higher than merely surviving."

"Oh, I'd love to. Unfortunately, not all of us have the luxury of marrying the king of the supernatural underworld and being whisked off to a beautiful castle in the country."

Jaci hated the bitterness in her voice, but what the hell was she supposed to say? Charley might've had a rough past, but now she was a vampire queen, cherished and loved, protected, part of a family that would do anything for her. She could afford to aim higher than survival.

Jaci didn't have that luxury.

"That's fair." Charley reached into the garnish dish behind the bar for another lime, squeezing it into her drink. "A bullshit copout, but fair."

"Copout?" Jaci laughed, a hollow and bitter sound that would've made her sad if she'd had time for wallowing. "So you got the fairytale happily-ever-after with a vampire who worships the ground you walk on. Congrats, girl, but life doesn't always work out like that for the rest of us."

"Are you kidding me?" Anger flared again in Charley's eyes. She pointed at Gabriel, who was now at the other end of the bar conferring with one of his vampire goons. "That vampire, for all his flaws, is in capital-L Love with you. You'd have to be lobotomized not to see it."

Jaci's cheeks flamed at the insinuation, but she forced herself to stand her ground. "Even if that were true, which—"

"Oh, it's totally true."

"—which it *isn't*... Do you seriously think that's enough? That being in capital-L Love is so damn easy, everything else just falls into place?"

"Let me tell you something, Jaci. Love is the *only* easy thing. It's the rest of it that makes it feel impossible—all that messy, complicated shit we pile on because we think we don't deserve to be happy. Because we can't imagine that someone could see all the worst parts of us and still want to hold us at night and cook us breakfast in the morning and just... just fucking *be* there. And if you think Dorian and I didn't go through our share of complicated shit, well... Get me drunk enough one night, and I'll tell you some stories that'll make your head spin." She drained the rest of her drink, then lowered the glass and cringed. "Sorry. Was that insensitive? I didn't mean 'head spin' in a demonic, exorcist kind of way. I meant the metaphorical way. Wait, your head doesn't *literally* spin, right?"

"Wow," Jaci deadpanned. "A gorgeous vampire queen *and* a comedienne? Watch out, world!"

Charley laughed, easing the last of the lingering tension between them.

"Look, Charley," Jaci said. "I appreciate the pep talk almost as much as I appreciate you not killing me. I just don't understand why you're trying so hard. The Redthornes are your family—I get it. But I'm… I'm just the enemy they've got on retainer to bring down a succubus and break a curse so the rest of you can get on with your lives. You don't need to go out of your way to be nice to me. You don't even have to talk to me."

Charley's eyes filled with something far worse than her earlier anger.

Pity.

"Is that what you think?" she asked, her voice soft, a little crease appearing between her eyebrows. "That Gabriel sees you as a means to an end?"

Jaci's eyes blurred with tears, and she turned away, rearranging liquor bottles on the shelves just to avoid Charley's gaze.

There was a time—just a couple of nights ago, actually—when Jaci would've said hell no. When she believed that maybe, just maybe, despite their hostile beginnings, she and Gabriel had a shot at building something real. The holding-each-other-at-night, cooking-breakfast-in-the-morning, just-being-there kind of real Charley was talking about.

But that ship had sailed, crashed, and sunk harder than

the Titanic, and no amount of "aiming higher" was going to salvage *that* wreckage.

"Deep down, I think you know how Gabriel *really* feels about you," Charley finally said, "so I won't belabor it. But speaking for myself... I'm talking to you because I *want* to talk to you, Jaci. I meant what I said the other night—I know what it's like when you're stuck between a rock and those flaming shit sandwiches."

Jaci laughed, finally turning around to face her again. "I think you're mixing metaphors."

"It's a gift," she said with a grin. Then, her smile softening, "I don't care what you've done, what you're ashamed of, or what sins you think you have to atone for. All that is in the past. If you tell me right now, honestly, that you want to be my friend—that you want to be part of this family no matter how messy, complicated, *and* flaming our piles of shit may be—then I'm willing to give you another chance."

Emotion welled in her chest.

Was this woman for real?

"But... why?" Jaci asked. "Why would you do that?"

Charley pulled out her phone and swiped to a photo, then handed the phone to Jaci.

"Your sister," Jaci said, recognizing the perky blonde woman in the shot, her face smushed up against Charley's like the pair couldn't bear to be separated. "She's adorable."

"She is. And smart, and hilarious, and seriously in love with Aiden, though she still won't admit it."

Jaci smiled. "Yeah, I may have heard something about that."

"Well, thanks to the fact that I'm a vampire—marrying the vampire *king*, no less—my little sister now has one foot in our world and one foot in her own. I can't always keep her safe, but I have to believe we can do better than tearing each other's throats out and lighting each other on fire. *All* of us—humans and supernaturals alike. You asked me why I want to give you a chance? That's the truth of it."

Jaci handed back the phone. "And here I thought you vamped out on a few innocents and needed a refill on your Karma points."

"Um... You're kinda rusty at this whole friend thing, huh?"

"Maybe a little. Let me try again." Jaci cleared her throat, flashed an exaggerated wink, and said, "Buy you another drink, friend?"

Charley grinned. "*Now* you're getting the hang of it."

"I'm a quick study."

"Perfect. That means we can skip the rest of the lectures and threats and officially move on to the fun stuff."

Jaci laughed, and this time, it wasn't hollow. The sound of it surprised her—lighter, somehow. Almost... almost happy. Hopeful.

If you tell me right now, honestly, that you want to be my friend—that you want to be part of this family...

Was it even possible? To be part of a family that chose you because they actually wanted you and cared about you, rather than one that created you with violence and manipulation, twisting you into some kind of monster to further their own power?

Every single one of Jaci's instincts, honed over years of torture and pain, screamed out the same answer.

No, it isn't *possible, you stupid girl. It's a trap. It's always a trap. What else could it be?*

There were a lot of things it could be, Jaci realized. A lot of terrible things, sure—but there was an equally strong chance those things could be amazing too.

Maybe she didn't have to figure it all out just yet. To run it through the filters of her fucked-up past or try to predict how it would turn out in the future. Right now, maybe it was enough to appreciate what she had in *this* moment—the possibility of a new friend. A group of vampires working to help her take down the demon that had cast a shadow over her entire life. And, as painful as it was to admit, a man she'd fallen in love with.

No matter if it ever turned into a real relationship, no matter how long that relationship lasted—five minutes, a year, a lifetime—loving someone was its own reward, even if it *was* destined to crash and burn.

For the first time since she arrived in New York City, a weight fell away from Jaci's heart, making room for the possibility that she actually *belonged* somewhere. That she might not have to leave it all behind after all.

Grabbing a bottle of top-shelf whiskey, Jaci poured them each a shot.

"To the fun stuff," she said, lifting her glass, and Charley rose from her barstool and followed suit, both of them grinning as they clinked glasses and polished off the drinks.

No sooner had Jaci set down her glass did the air change

—a hot and sudden shift that crackled with a strange electric charge, like the warning of a storm you'd never be able to outrun.

Something was coming.

Across the crowd of customers lined up at the bar, Jaci sought out Gabriel, their gazes locking instantly. He blurred into her space and grabbed her, crushing her against his chest, mouth close to her ear.

"We need to get out of here," he whispered urgently, but it was too late.

The obsidian mirrors lining the club's elegant walls shifted from gleaming black to a bright, bone-chilling red. *Blood* red. Viansa's face shone out from every one of them, a beacon of terror.

Her red lips parted in a menacing grin, and when she finally spoke, the entire club fell deadly silent.

"Hello, my loves. Have you missed me?"

CHAPTER SIXTEEN

Viansa's image vanished from the mirrors, but the damage was done.

Her very voice had cast a dark enchantment, freezing the entire club full of supernaturals in place, locking their minds and bodies in stasis. For as long as the spell lasted, they'd be aware of nothing. When Viansa broke the enchantment, they'd awaken, feeling only a vague sense that something was off.

It was an old trick—one she used to play on Jaci when she was just a toddler. Back then, Viansa would relocate her to different hell realms before breaking the spell, confusing and terrifying her at every turn.

Now, Jaci was the only one who remained conscious and mobile.

Light spilled in through the entrance, and she pulled out of Gabriel's frozen embrace to see Viansa, awash in a golden glow, sauntering into Obsidian like a wayward Hollywood starlet.

The succubus was draped in a sleek black satin dress that matched her glamorous hair and hugged every curve, a stark contrast to her pale skin and red lips. Tall silver heels, a stunning diamond choker, and a vintage red leather handbag finished off the look. The effect was breathtaking —the perfect mix of haute couture and dastardly horror-movie villainess.

"Shot of Fireball, please," Viansa purred, shoving a vampire patron off a barstool and taking a seat. "Developed a taste for them last night at NYU. Now *those* boys know how to throw a party."

Not sure what else to do, Jaci grabbed the cinnamon-flavored whiskey from the shelf and poured the shot. "Nine dollars."

"Seriously? You're making your sister buy her own drinks?"

Jaci held out her hand, saying nothing.

"*Someone's* getting a little big for her britches." Viansa reached into her purse, fishing out a twenty and handing it over. "Keep the change."

Where she'd gotten the cash, Jaci had no idea, but she wasn't surprised to see it—just like the outfit. Viansa was resourceful and adaptable and had a way of persuading anyone to do anything.

Case in point: mass public orgies.

Jaci slid her hands into her back pockets and leaned against the liquor shelves, mind racing to come up with a plan. With the entire crew completely immobilized, a physical attack was out of the question, and a magical one probably wouldn't get her anywhere either. Her best shot—assuming Viansa wasn't going to roast her the instant she finished her drink—would be to pump the demon for intel, hoping she let a few juicy tidbits slip.

Tidbits they could later use to nail the bitch to the wall.

The thought infused her with a deep sense of purpose.

"Done with your tour of the city?" Jaci asked. "You should head back home. I'm sure Mom misses you."

Viansa practically snorted. *"Please.* That demonic sideshow probably doesn't even know I'm gone."

Beneath the insult, Jaci detected the barest hint of rejection in her voice.

Good, she thought. If Viansa and their mother were on one of their many "breaks," maybe this scheme was all Viansa's doing, which meant one less original demon for her and the others to worry about.

"Besides, I love it here," Viansa said. "I've met the most amazing people! So ambitious. So eager to please. So… *insatiable.*"

Her smile fell, lips pursing into a sad little pout.

"So what's the problem?" Jaci asked. "Is that not what you want?"

"Every human I fuck becomes instantly obsessed with me and *dies* from all the sex. Like, literally. Sometimes right in the middle of it." She rolled her eyes and downed her shot, leaving a lipstick print on the glass. "It's *so* boring."

Jaci bit back the urge to ask how high the body count

had gotten. After yesterday's initial wave of orgies, they hadn't heard anything unusual in the news or on social media—just endless recaps about the unexplained "mass hysteria" that had momentarily gripped New York. But Viansa could've killed dozens of humans since then, their bodies yet undiscovered.

"Maybe you should find a supernatural plaything instead?" Jaci said, forcing a casual shrug. "Might last a bit longer in bed. You'd have to unfreeze them, though."

She narrowed her eyes and wagged a finger. "Nice try."

"Worth a shot."

"Jay, if you wanted your pals to remain conscious tonight, maybe you should've cast a spell to protect them? I mean, *you're* the witch-mutt, but that just seems like Magic 101 to me."

"Thanks. I'll keep it in mind for next time."

Viansa toyed with the shot glass, rolling it in a circle on the bar. "Truth be told, I considered banging a vampire, maybe a shifter or two, but supernaturals aren't as docile as humans. Takes longer to break them in, if you get my meaning." She sighed, then righted her glass and gestured for a refill. "Trade-offs, right? Besides, as much fun as I'm having in this crazy-ass city, I can't lose sight of the mission."

"Mission?" Jaci poured her another shot, this time waving away the offered cash, hoping to keep in Viansa's good graces. To keep the bitch talking.

Viansa was manipulative and clever and scary-powerful, but she was also a vain little asshole. If anything was to be her epic downfall, that was likely it.

"I'm not just here for a pleasure cruise, Lab Rat," she said. "I need to find a way to smash open those hell gates for good." She downed the second shot, then grinned, her eyes glinting in a way that sent waves of panic rolling down Jaci's spine. "And I've had the most brilliant idea ever! *You're* going to help me."

"Your dark-mage pals aren't pulling their weight?"

"No, the mages are great. They do everything I ask— sometimes even before I ask it. It's just… This particular project is a bit beyond them."

"Beyond *them*, but not me?" Jaci laughed. "You just lectured me on Magic 101. How the fuck do you expect me to mess with hell magic?"

"Hell is your home. It's in your blood."

"I haven't been there in years. And even when I *was* home, I could never cast the sort of magic you and Mom wanted."

"I know! Believe me, when you first left us, I never would've thought you'd be capable of something so… so big. But look! You've survived all this time on your own. Snagged yourself a royal vampire super-hottie. Something tells me you've still got a few more tricks up your sleeve." Viansa plucked a cherry from the garnish tray and ate it, pit, stem, and all. "Besides, it'll be fun! Jaci and Vi, together again. Just like old times."

"Old times. Right. Like the old time you tied me to a post and sprayed me with acid? Or maybe the old time you slit my throat and portaled me to the Salt Flats, turning me into bait for the demon vultures? Or… I know! The old time you force-fed me a hundred live centipedes. Ahh, those were the days." Jaci's stomach roiled with nausea at the memories of all the tortures her sister had inflicted, all the realms of hell she'd forced her to endure, all the pain.

But Viansa waved it all away as if it were no more than a bit of sibling rivalry. "Mother's healers patched you right up. No harm, no foul. Seriously, Jay. Holding on to the past is the surest way to get stuck there. Just as any of the poor souls in the pits."

Fury sizzled in her veins. Jaci couldn't even *pretend* to tolerate her. Not even for the intel they so desperately needed. "If I had the means, I'd kill you where you stand."

"Now you're just being dramatic. Look, this will be good for us. A way to reconnect. Start fresh. Besides, once the demons take over up here and I become queen, I'll need a right hand. Prove your loyalty now, and the world could be your oyster. That's a thing, right? The world is your oyster? Or is it lobster?" She wrinkled her nose and shrugged. "Either way, it's yours."

Is she fucking high?

Jaci folded her arms over her chest. "And if I refuse? I'm not big on seafood."

"Hmm." Viansa tapped a black-lacquered fingernail against her lips. "Let's consider how that would play out. First, *you'd* be like, 'No, Viansa. I *refuse* to help you, even though you're my flesh-and-blood sister. Sadly, I never learned the concept of loyalty, so I'm afraid you're on your own.' Then *I'd* get *super* pissed, and I'd go, 'Okay, Lab Rat. Have it your way.' And then—this is the best part—*I'd* go…" Her grin stretched wide, the sight of it sending Jaci's stomach into free fall. Glancing behind Jaci, she said, "Gabe, honey? You look absolutely famished. When was the last time you fed?"

She wasn't just role-playing. She was speaking directly to Gabriel, whose hollow gaze had suddenly locked onto Viansa's, his fangs flashing behind a hungry snarl.

"*Don't*," Jaci warned, trying to position herself in front of Gabriel, as if she could shield him from her sister's evil machinations. "Whatever you're thinking, just—"

Viansa snapped her fingers, and Gabriel broke out of the freeze, sidestepping Jaci and blurring right over the bar.

"Snack time, sweetie," Viansa crooned. "Better not waste a drop!"

With neither hesitation nor emotion, Gabriel grabbed a red-headed fox shifter seated on the barstool next to Viansa and bit into her artery, sending a spray of blood across his face. After the first taste, he latched on harder and sucked, a deep groan of pleasure reverberating through his chest, mixing with the sound of his incessant slurping.

Jaci climbed over the bar and tried to intervene, begging him to stop, but it was useless. He was too far gone, too focused on his task, too caught up in Viansa's thrall. When she tried to physically pull him away from the poor woman, he turned and growled at her, then went right back to his meal.

Moments later, the woman slumped forward, completely unaware, completely drained.

Gabriel stood stock-still, a robot awaiting his next command.

"Fuck. *Fuck!*" Jaci reached for the woman's neck, pushing through the warm slick of blood in search of a pulse.

Nothing.

"She's dead," she whispered.

"Uh, yeah? That's what happens when a vampire drains you." Viansa rolled her eyes. "Honestly, kiddo. You'd think you'd have that part figured out by now, considering you're fucking the guy. But… whatever. It's not my job anymore to school you on the harsh realities of life. I lost that privilege the day you left hell."

Through gritted teeth, Jaci said, "Fine."

"Fine, what?"

"I'll do it. I'll help you break the gates."

"Really?" Viansa bounced on her barstool, clapping her hands like a little girl. "Like, *really* really?"

"Really really," Jaci said, but Viansa was already frowning again.

"I *want* to believe you. I'm just not sure you're fully on board with this."

"I am," she said, knowing there was no other choice. "I swear it. Just stop with the torture show, and I'm all yours."

Viansa glanced at her fingernails, then back to Jaci, clearly unconvinced.

"I don't know, Jay. Maybe we need *one* more example, just to drive the point home. Pun intended." She reached into her purse, eyebrows waggling.

Jaci recognized that new light in her sister's eyes, a particular joy that only burned in her cruelest moments.

"It's fine," Jaci repeated, desperate to regain control. "I said I'd help you and I meant it. We can start right now. You don't have to—"

"Gabe, my little sugarplum? I need a *teensy*-weensy favor." Viansa pulled something out of her purse and tossed it to Gabe, who caught it easily.

It took Jaci a beat to realize what it was.

A stake. Sharp, wooden, deadly.

Sheer terror ran through Jaci's limbs, paralyzing her.

"There's only room for *one* queen in this city." With a menacing, blood-red grin, Viansa pointed at Charley, who'd been standing in front of the bar several feet down, frozen in place since Viansa's arrival. Then, her eyes hardening right along with her voice, she said, "Take that vampire bitch down. *Now*."

In that dreadful moment, as Gabriel tightened his grip on the stake and stepped forward, life flashed before Jaci's eyes.

Not her own, but Charley's.

She blinked and saw Dorian and Charley on their wedding day, glowing with so much love and happiness they rivaled the sun. She blinked again, and there was Dorian, kneeling in the dirt and weeping over a headstone, inconsolable and lost without his queen. Another blink and Sasha appeared, her once-bright eyes dim and dark as she wandered the halls of Ravenswood, calling out for a sister who'd never answer. On the last blink, Jaci saw her new friend Charley—the vampire queen who'd given her a second chance, the woman who'd seen past her many mistakes and offered understanding instead of scorn—collapse in a pile of ash.

Every heartbreaking image rushed through her mind in a heartbeat as Gabriel marched toward his victim. *Viansa's* victim.

Ten seconds till impact.

Five.

Three.

Jaci didn't blink again. Didn't speak. Didn't think.

She just dove.

CHAPTER SEVENTEEN

Blood. The taste of it, the scent. It flooded Gabriel's senses, shocking him back to consciousness.

Awareness barreled into his mind with the force of a planetary collision, splitting his skull and wringing the breath from his lungs.

He sucked in a deep gulp of air, the pain in his head slowly fading, shapes and colors coming into sharp focus.

Jacinda stood in front of Charlotte, eyes wide, breath shallow, blouse soaked in blood. It took him a beat to notice the stake protruding from her mid-section. Another beat to find his own bloody fingers wrapped around the end of it as if he'd been the one to…

Fucking hell.

Memories flashed through his mind, a horror movie on high speed.

Viansa. The innocent fox shifter he'd drained. His near-attack on Charlotte, thwarted by Jacinda.

"Jacinda," he breathed, shock and anguish squeezing his heat.

"You're... back." She forced smile, faint and bloody, then swayed. He caught her before she fell, scooping her into his arms.

"Holy fuck!" Charlotte gasped, awakening along with all the others, her eyes wide as she took in the gory sight.

"Call Colin and Isabelle," he barked. "Tell them to meet me in my office at once. Tell Colin to bring his medical bag."

"I... Right. On it." Blinking away the momentary confusion, Charlotte whipped out her phone, and Gabriel blurred Jacinda up to his office.

As carefully as he could manage, he laid her on the desk, shoving everything else to the floor. Guilt and terror gnawed through his chest, devouring the last of his shock. The thudding of his heart was so wild and erratic, he thought it might explode.

"What have I done?" he whispered. "Bloody hell, Jacinda. I'm so sorry." He tried to examine the wound, but he couldn't see anything past the blood, and he didn't dare remove the stake. For all he knew, that hunk of wood was the only thing holding her together.

"Viansa," she choked out, voice wet and strangled. She lifted a trembling hand to Gabriel's face, her blue eyes dimming, her mouth turning soft and sad. "Her fault. Not... yours."

"Shh. Don't talk. Colin's on his way." Gabriel looked

over his shoulder through the open door, but there was no sign of his brother or the elder witch. No sign of help.

Where the fuck are they?

He backed away, intending to check the hallway for any sign of them, but Jacinda grabbed his arm and drew him close.

"Don't," she said. "Don't leave me."

He forced a smile, smoothing the blood-soaked hair away from her face, trying to hide the tremor in his hands. "Never."

"Promise?"

"I'm right here, little moonflower."

"Tired."

"I know, love. But you need to stay with me. Keep me company."

She smiled, her eyes glazed, lids heavy. Every breath she drew became shallower than the last.

"Are you immortal?" he blurted out, fear pounding in his head. His heart. Every part of him.

Fuck. Why the hell hadn't he thought to ask sooner?

"Don't... know. Never... almost died before." She tried to laugh, but the movement sent a spasm of pain through her body.

Gabriel grabbed her hand and held tight, trying to work out the answer on his own. "Witches aren't immortal, and neither are demonic vessels, but demonic essences are. Unless they're exorcised, of course. Your father is a mage, so he wouldn't be. But your mother is an original—definitely immortal." He walked backward through time, desperately trying to remember anything he might've learned about genetics from Colin, from their father's medical books, from the damn television, but nothing came to him.

"Gabriel, I need… to tell you… I…" She coughed, blood leaking from her mouth, a dark streak against pale lips.

No. I'm not letting you die tonight. Not like this, for fuck's sake.

"Hey," he said softly, brushing a kiss over her brow. "You can tell me anything you'd like later. Anything at all. Bad jokes, your dirtiest fantasies…" This earned him a small smile, and it buoyed him. "Actually, I'd take the fantasies over the jokes, but—"

"Ladies' choice," she whispered, and Gabriel nodded.

"For you, always."

"Sleep now." Her voice was faint, her eyelids fluttering closed.

"Not yet, moonflower." He kissed her again, soft as a breeze. "You've still got a few hours left on your shift."

The ghost of a smile returned to her lips, but it fell away just as quickly.

"Jacinda," he said. "Jace. Wake up, love. I need you to wake up."

She stirred again, barely clinging to consciousness.

"That's it." Gabriel stroked her hair. "Good girl. Just a little longer, and—"

Charlotte burst into the office, breathless, joining him at the desk. "They're almost here—they were both still in the city. Five more minutes tops. How is she?"

Gabriel shook his head, unable to speak through the grief and panic rising in his throat.

"Fuck, Gabriel. Jaci... she saved my life." Charlotte's voice quavered, a tear sliding down her cheek. "I'm so fucking sorry. I didn't know. I..."

"I know. It's not your fault." Gabriel wrapped a hand around the back of Charlotte's neck and squeezed, and together they held their silent vigil, waiting.

The span of those five minutes felt like fucking forever, and by the time Colin and Isabelle arrived, supplies in hand, Jacinda was pale and listless, no longer speaking at all, her pulse faint. The two experts swept in and got to work examining the wound, taking vitals, each speaking their own language—medical jargon, magical, nothing Gabriel could follow.

There in the corner, just behind the desk where the woman who'd stolen his heart lay bleeding to death, the child who'd haunted him for centuries flickered into view. She stared openly, her eyes as empty as ever, the weight of her silent accusations more than he could bear.

If she dies, he wanted to tell her, *I'm going with her.*

He knew it as certainly as he knew his own name. Of all the guilt he carried, all the vile things he'd done as a man and a vampire both, all the regrets that haunted his nightmares and burned through his chest with every waking breath, *this* would be the last. The death knell for a vicious monster who didn't deserve to walk this earth. A monster who should've been banished to hell the moment he'd made his very first kill.

Good, the child seemed to say. *That's where you belong.*

Finally, the doctor and the witch came to an agreement —the stake had missed the heart, but still nicked something vital, and Viansa's dark magic seemed to be making the whole situation worse. Blood welled up around the wound, black and viscous.

"So do something!" Gabriel roared, his voice raw, his body buzzing with adrenaline and fury. "Fix her!"

"We're doing everything we can," Colin said softly. Then, looking to Charlotte, his eyes imploring, "Get him out of here."

Charlotte nodded and reached for Gabriel's arm. Reluctantly, he allowed himself to be led out, closing the office door behind him, hoping like hell the very last memory of his little moonflower wouldn't be soaked in blood.

CHAPTER EIGHTEEN

The vampires stood on the balcony overlooking the main level, hundreds of revelers downstairs caught up in their endless partying as if they hadn't just been completely mind-fucked by a succubus.

"Your man Enzo took care of the fox shifter," Charlotte said. "He was quick and quiet—made it look like she'd just had too much to drink."

Gabriel nodded, guilt tying him up inside.

That poor fucking woman…

Keeping his attention on the crowd downstairs, he said, "They don't remember a damn thing. That bitch imprisoned us all in a nightmare, and for them, it's as if it never even happened."

Charlotte ran her hands over her blood-soaked jacket—Jacinda's blood, he realized—and sighed. "I was talking with Isabelle this morning, and she told me succubi have incredible powers of mind control. This kind of spell? You and I shouldn't be able to remember it, either."

"Same thing happened when she showed up in my bedroom and hijacked my mind. I remembered everything. But that time, I was able to break out of her thrall. Jacinda told me even Viansa was shocked by it." He rubbed his forehead, his headache coming back with a vengeance. "How is any of this possible?"

"I don't understand it any more than you do. As a human, I was immune to vampire compulsion. I'm guessing this is related. But that doesn't explain your situation."

"I just... Tonight was different, Charlotte. Not just a vision planted in my mind. She *owned* me, and this time, I wasn't even aware of it. I don't understand how she was able to overtake me so completely that I... that I was willing to kill an innocent woman at her command. I very nearly killed *you*. I... I staked Jacinda as if she meant nothing to me, and now she's..." His voice broke, and he turned away, unable to face the pain in Charlotte's eyes, a mirror to his own. "How the fuck are we supposed to defeat her if we can't even see her coming? If she can control us so completely, so invasively?"

"I don't know, Gabriel. But if my experience with the Redthornes has taught me anything, it's that you guys *always* find a way to protect the people you love."

Silently, she looped her arm through his and rested her head against his shoulder, both of them clearly grateful for the company.

Gabriel didn't know how much time passed, he and Charlotte lost in their own private hells, the partiers carrying on downstairs, laughter and music floating up to the heavens. There'd been no word from the other side of the door, which he hoped was a good thing. If the wound was fatal, he reasoned, she would've died by now, and someone would've come to deliver the news.

Colin and Isabelle were just taking their time, making sure they patched her up properly. That's all it was. Nothing to fear.

"Jaci's fine," Charlotte said suddenly, as if she'd read his thoughts. "You think one little stake to the chest can take *her* down? You and I both know the woman is scrappy as hell."

Gabriel allowed a soft chuckle. "She's definitely a fighter, that one."

"She'd have to be to put up with *your* bullshit."

At that, Gabriel turned to her and smiled, grateful for the distraction. "*My* bullshit? Whatever do you mean, Ms. D'Amico?"

She nudged his arm with her elbow. "You know what I mean."

"No, I'd really like to hear your thoughts on the matter. Since you're apparently the expert on my so-called bullshit."

"Are we confessing now? Okay, fine. The first time I met you—at the fundraiser? I thought you were the *biggest* asshole."

"Wait. Are you referring to the night my brothers and I

caught you and Dorian *in flagrante delicto* in the guest house, dodging a party he was supposedly hosting? *That night?*"

"Hey!" She smacked his chest. "Don't deflect! We're talking about *your* bullshit, not mine."

"Right. Carry on."

"I looked at all of you lined up together outside the guest house, side by side in your tuxes, no idea that you were vampires. And I thought, *wow*. Of all the Redthorne brothers, Gabriel has the most massive stick up his ass."

"Debatable."

"Suspected, demonstrated, and proven many times over. *But...*"

"But?"

She shrugged, and the teasing sparkle in her eyes turned serious. "But then you helped Dorian take out those vampires who tried to kill me, and you helped me destroy my shithead uncle and get my sister back, and now you're... I don't know. Growing on me, I guess. In an asshole kind of way, but still."

"I'll take it as a compliment. In an asshole kind of way, but still." Gabriel put an arm around her, once again glad of her company. "You know, I recall a night not so long ago when *your* life was in Colin's hands, and my brother was crawling the damn walls thinking you'd die before he confessed his love. Not that he'd admit it to us, mind you. It was written all over his face from the very start. Sappy bastard."

She poked him in the ribs. "There's two life lessons there, my friend."

"And I'm sure you're keen to share them with me."

She turned to look at him again, a note of seriousness lingering in her eyes. "When you love someone, tell them. Don't worry about what anyone else thinks or how crazy it seems or how high the odds are stacked against you. Don't even worry about whether they'll return the feelings."

Gabriel forced a smile, hoping to hide the fire burning in his heart. "Sounds dangerous."

"Oh, it's totally dangerous. But if you keep it all locked up, every moment you spend with that person is just perpetuating a lie. What's the point?"

He drew a breath to deny it, but there was no use. Women always seemed to have this shit figured out. She'd probably predicted his feelings for Jacinda that first fucking night at Bloodbath, long before he could even admit the possibility to himself.

"So what's the second lesson?" he said instead.

"Loving a vampire comes with a lot of risks. Especially loving a Redthorne vampire."

Gabriel nodded, fresh pain searing his chest. In a defeated whisper, he said, "I'm not sure why she'd ever take such a risk."

Charlotte stretched up on her toes and kissed his cheek, then pulled back with a soft smile, her eyes shining. "Because you're worth it."

A swell of affection for the woman rose in his chest. "Dorian's lucky to have you, Charlotte D'Amico."

She wiped away a tear that'd slipped out and laughed. "Damn straight he is. And you're lucky to have Jacinda. So please do us all a favor and don't fuck it up, or I'll have to tear out *your* throat."

"Noted. You really like her, don't you?"

"Meh," Charlotte teased. "I just don't want to redo the seating chart for the reception. I'd have to switch you with Aiden, and then Sasha would throw a fit and it would turn into a whole *thing*... Better for everyone if you just behave yourself and—"

The office door opened, calling them both to rapt attention.

Colin looked like he'd aged a decade in the span of an hour, but when he finally met Gabriel's eyes, a soft smile touched his lips, and Gabriel almost wept with relief.

"Jacinda's going to be okay," Colin said. "Her body has extraordinary healing properties—just needed a bit of encouragement. Well, that and Isabelle's magic, along with some very strong painkillers."

"Can I take her home?" Gabriel asked.

"Of course. But..." Colin touched his shoulder, his eyes holding a warning. "She needs rest, Gabriel. And no added stress. I know everyone's working hard to stop Viansa— and tonight only proves how imperative that is. But Jacinda needs time to fully heal."

"I won't let her lift so much as a cocktail shaker, brother."

Beside him, Charlotte squeezed his arm. "I'm going to

call Dorian and let him know what's going on. Are you okay?"

He covered her hand with his and nodded. "Thanks in large part to your grade-A distraction skills, yes."

They shared another smile, something raw and genuine passing between them. A new understanding, perhaps. A familial closeness arrived at grudgingly, painfully, but nevertheless real.

"Tell Jaci I'm coming over first thing tomorrow," she said. "I'll bring breakfast and stuff for mani/pedis."

"Don't you have to work?" he asked. Charlotte had a marketing job at FierceConnect, Dorian and Aiden's social gaming company. "I've heard your boss is kind of a dick. Not quite the asshole his younger brother is, but close."

Charlotte laughed again, the sound of it adding levity to a situation that had nearly gutted him.

"I'll make it up to him," she said. "Just don't forget to tell Jaci I'm coming. Girls' day or bust, okay?"

Gabriel promised he'd relay the message, then headed in to see his woman.

The child in the stained dress was thankfully gone.

Jacinda was still lying on the desk, but they'd cut away the blouse and bandaged her mid-section, all traces of blood eradicated, her breathing deep and even. Gabriel shrugged out of his suit jacket, and Colin and Isabelle helped him carefully wrap her up, situating her in his arms so he could carry her home.

"She saved Charlotte's life," he whispered, staring down at her pale lips, the hair plastered against her face. She was

SARAH PIPER

sleeping peacefully now, looking young and untroubled, but nothing could be further from the truth.

She'd nearly died tonight.

At *his* hand.

The realization arrowed through his heart all over again, shredding him.

"She did," Colin said. "It was reckless and brave, and when she wakes up tomorrow, I'll need to decide what comes first: the gratitude or the lecture. Believe me, brother, she'll be getting both from me."

He smiled, but Gabriel could no longer share in the humor. "The stake... I would have incinerated Charlotte. My brother's future wife. His queen. My sister-in-law."

"It wasn't your fault, Gabriel. Viansa—"

"Jacinda jumped in front of her," he said, tightening his hold on her. "Why would she *do* that?"

"I suspect it's because she's got a good heart."

"A heart I very nearly skewered."

"Ours is not a peaceful existence. It never will be." Colin clapped him on the shoulder, his eyes as soft and kind as his voice. "Make peace with *that*, brother, or you'll end up following in our father's footsteps, straight to the grave."

164

CHAPTER NINETEEN

The rest of the week passed in restless agony as Jaci waited to hear from Gabriel—the kind of agony that couldn't be chased away with one of Colin's painkillers or a few stiff drinks.

Her physical wounds had healed quickly. But her heart? That was another story.

Why the fuck had he been avoiding her?

Since the attack on Obsidian that'd left one shifter dead and Jaci herself as close to the Big Sleep as she'd ever ventured, Colin had visited her twice each day, monitoring her vitals, checking on her progress. Last night, he'd finally removed her bandages and declared her eighty percent back to normal.

Charley had shown up that very first morning with enough food to feed an army, enough cosmetics to treat every witch in the city to a luxurious spa day, and all the streaming service passwords she possessed, as if she were determined to not only show her gratitude for the save, but to make up for all the years Jaci had spent without a real girlfriend.

Since then, she'd dropped in on Jaci every day during her lunch break, bringing soup and sandwiches from a French place near her office in Tribeca, redoing Jaci's nails even though the original manicure hadn't even begun to chip.

Isabelle had also popped in regularly, brewing tea, swapping out new lore books and occult texts for the old, reading out passages she found relevant. They still hadn't zeroed in on anything concrete about binding succubi in general, let alone about Viansa specifically, but not for lack of trying.

After all the horror of Monday's attack, Jaci was still baffled about her sister's vanishing act. The moment she'd jumped in front of Charley and caught the pointy end of that stake, Viansa vanished. No ominous threats, no indication about what she wanted Jaci to do with the hell gates.

The only clue she'd left in her wake was the look in her eyes. Jaci only caught the barest glimpse of it before the stake pierced her flesh, but it was there, clear as the morning sun.

Fear. True, unadulterated fear.

She hadn't meant for Jaci to get hurt.

It was an unintentional show of her hand—one whose meaning Jaci hadn't quite deciphered—but one that could possibly give them a leg up in the fight. Viansa could make all the threats she wanted, but for now, it seemed Jaci would be spared the worst of her wrath.

She wished she could say the same for the others.

New worry turned over in her stomach, making her queasy. She knew Gabriel was physically okay—Colin and Charley had confirmed it. He was just busy with security, they'd said. Busy filling in for her at Obsidian. Busy chasing down false leads about Viansa's constantly-changing whereabouts, *But don't worry!* they'd said. *He sends his regards!*

Jaci nodded and smiled and pretended to be okay with it all, but deep down, she was a red-hot mess.

She fucking missed the asshole. Missed his wintergreen scent. Missed his intense, brooding gaze. Missed the looming mass of him as he crowded into her space. She even missed their bickering.

Her memories of that night were still a little hazy—the attack itself was clear, but the rest came to her in pieces, mostly in her dreams. Gabriel returning to himself, the look of horror on his face when he realized what'd happened. Gabriel, sweeping her into his office, soothing her as she drifted in and out of consciousness. Voices overhead, hands on her body, sudden relief from the pain. Strong arms holding her close, tucking her into bed. The press of soft, warm lips against her temple.

She had the same dream every night—Gabriel kneeling at her bedside, trailing his fingers through her hair, whispering distraught apologies as if any of this was his fault.

Sometimes the dreams felt so real, so visceral, she'd

awaken with a start, certain she could smell him. Certain she could feel his presence in the darkness. Certain she'd find him there, waiting for her to smile at him. To ask for another kiss.

But then she'd flick on the light, illuminating the same empty room, the same endless silence.

The same clawing heartache.

By the time the weekend hit, Jaci was absolutely *done* with moping around in the apartment, crawling the walls waiting for her vampire prince to show his stupidly handsome face. Even though Colin hadn't yet cleared her to return to work, on Friday night she made three important decisions.

One, she was showering, primping, and getting dressed up in her hottest ensemble.

Two, she was putting on her sultriest wine-colored lipstick.

And three, she was marching down to Obsidian, planting her hot little ass firmly behind the bar, and debuting a brand-new drink: The Flaming Phoenix, in honor of her triumphant return.

"Eat your heart out, dickhead," she said to her reflection in the mirror, smoothing the last errant curl into place. "This bitch is a fucking *snack*."

Then, tossing a few things into her purse and grabbing her coat, she headed for the door.

She opened it hard and fast, fully prepared for a verbal sparring match with the two vampire guards Gabriel had stationed in the hallway. They'd been positioned there all week, as unmoving and rock-solid as gargoyles, armed to the teeth with guns and stakes and something that looked terrifyingly like a rocket launcher.

But tonight when Jaci opened the door, she found only one vampire, armed not with weapons, but with two potted plants, their scent giving them away as readily as their bright green leaves.

Mentha spicata.

Mint.

CHAPTER TWENTY

"Gabriel," Jaci breathed, the taste of his name on her lips bringing tears to her eyes.

Seeing him there, awkwardly fumbling with the plants, his misty green gaze full of a vulnerability he'd never allowed her to see…

All her righteous anger blew away on a soft sigh.

Dickhead or not—*holy hell*, she'd missed him.

"Right, then," he announced, shuffling his feet like a nervous schoolboy reporting for detention. It was so out of character, she was beginning to doubt whether it was really Gabriel. Maybe a doppelgänger, or a shapeshifter, or—

"I brought you some mint." He thrust the plants toward her, but as soon as she reached for them, he snatched them back. "Wait, sorry. You shouldn't be lifting anything heavy."

"Potted plants? Not exactly moving pianos here, Prince."

"Why risk it?" Dragging his gaze up and down her curves, all decked out in leather and silk, he said, "I should come inside."

Yes, you should. Forget the plants and the excuses and awkwardness and just march into this apartment, haul me into your arms, tear off my clothes, and fuck me straight through the goddamn wall...

Jaci lifted her chin and shook out her hair, ignoring the machine-gun fire of her heartbeat. The heat pooling inconveniently between her thighs.

It's called dignity, girl. Have some.

"Actually, I was just heading out," she said.

"Out? But I've just... Where?"

"Obsidian, if you must know."

"Oh, I think not."

"*Excuse* me?"

He moved into her space, forcing her to step aside and let him pass or risk crushing the poor plants. "It's snowing, you're barely dressed, the bar is packed with miscreants, and you need to rest."

Is he fucking serious right now?

"Excuse me," she said again, following him back into the apartment, urging the embers of her anger back to life. "If I get any more rest, I'm going to need a coffin."

He set the plants on the table and sighed. "Jacinda, you're still recovering from a serious—"

"No. You don't get to do that. Not now."

"Do what?"

She tossed her purse and coat on a chair and folded her arms across her chest, glaring at him with every version of the evil eye she had in her arsenal. "Show up here acting like you know what I need. Like you're suddenly concerned about my well-being. You haven't even returned my calls or texts."

"I've been running around this city for days, looking for Viansa. Trying to parse through the intel Cole's getting from the warehouse. Trying to figure out our next move. I meant to call, but I—"

"That night was a horror show, Gabriel. An absolute horror show. And I've spent the last four days wondering if I did something wrong—some terrible thing I must've blocked out—even though everyone keeps telling me I'm some kind of badass for saving Charley."

"Badass is an understatement," he said. "I had to talk Dorian out of coming down here and throwing himself at your feet. He has a whole speech prepared—be warned."

He tried to smile, but Jaci shook her head, the fire inside her gathering more heat.

She didn't want his smile any more than she wanted his brother's speech.

"Jacinda," he said, his voice softening. "Why would you think you'd done something wrong?"

"You didn't come," she blurted out.

"But… Colin assured me you were fine. He and Isabelle, Charlotte… I knew you were in good hands."

"They've all been amazing, and I'm grateful for that—more than I can ever express. But of all the people taking care of me, the one I *most* needed to see—the one I just really fucking missed—was gone."

Gabriel's face fell, guilt clouding his eyes. "Jace, I—"

"Look, I know things between us aren't exactly… I mean, I lied to you about my life and my sister, I put you and your family at risk, and you already hated witches and demons more than most people hate spiders and root canals, but—"

"This isn't about—"

"But even with all that… It's not like I'm expecting your forgiveness or your trust, but I thought we'd at least gotten to… I don't know. A better place, maybe. A place where if I got hurt, you'd come and check on me once or twice. Hell, even Maritza and the servers at Obsidian sent cookies and balloons."

"I brought mint!" he exclaimed, gesturing at the plants as if they made up for his absence. His disregard.

But even Gabriel knew it was a flimsy attempt. He lowered his hands and closed his eyes, cursing.

"You ghosted me," she said softly. "I almost died, and the man I… You weren't there, Gabriel. What was I supposed to think?"

Tears sprung to her eyes, undoubtedly ruining her perfectly gorgeous makeup.

So much for dignity.

"Is that really what you think?" Gabriel asked, hurt and confusion filling his eyes. He stepped closer, bringing with him the scent she loved so much. The scent she'd missed. "That I ghosted you?"

Jaci nodded and lowered her gaze, unable to find any more words, unable to bear the weight of the inexplicable pain in his eyes.

She was the one who'd been hurt and ignored. Gabriel had no business acting like—

"Jacinda," he breathed, cupping her face and resting his forehead against hers. The touch was so unexpected, so intimate, it made her gasp. "When I saw you bleeding that night... When I saw what I'd done to you... I have been bloody *beside* myself with worry ever since, tormented by things I cannot even begin to voice. I thought I'd lost you. I thought I'd..."

He trailed off into a deep sigh that whispered against her mouth, and she closed her eyes, the tears slipping silently down her cheeks.

In a broken whisper, she said, "Then why weren't you here?"

"Oh, little moonflower. I *was* here." Still holding her face, he drew back, pressing a kiss to each eyebrow, his thumbs gently wiping her tears. "Night after night, I watched you sleep. I knelt at your bedside and held your hand, trying to convince myself I could still keep you safe. That I'd never again allow myself to be put into a position where I might hurt you."

She opened her eyes and searched his face, trying to find a lie that simply wasn't there.

"I thought I was dreaming," she whispered. "I felt your presence, but when I woke up, you were always gone."

"I couldn't bear the thought of looking into your beautiful blue eyes and seeing them filled with hatred." A sad smile touched his lips, and he tucked a lock of hair behind her ear. "I'm a coward. Even tonight, I wasn't planning on staying. I thought I could give you the mint, exchange a few pleasantries, and be on my way. But then I saw your smile, your eyes, and I couldn't walk away from you."

His words wrapped around her heart, smoothing over some of the cracks. But the ache in his voice was still so raw, so sharp.

Jaci shook her head. "I could never hate you, Gabriel. None of it was your fault. As far as I'm concerned, Viansa's the one who staked me. *She's* the fucking coward."

He flinched at her words, closing his eyes and pressing his lips together, his body suddenly tense.

"It wasn't your fault," she said again. "I'm hurt that you didn't call or visit me, but I could never hate you for what my sister did."

"It's not just your sister. It's... Bloody hell, Jace. Don't you get it?" He lowered his hands to her shoulders and met her gaze once more. "Whenever one of Chernikov's demons hurt you, I knew exactly what I had to do. Wasn't even a conscious thought—just instinct. Hunt him down, torture him, end his existence. Same with the Dark Flame mages. They hurt you, threatened to kill you, and—"

"And you slaughtered them. No questions asked."

Gabriel nodded. "So you see my dilemma."

"No. All I see is a vampire blaming himself for the actions of a deranged succubus. And if you think I'm going to let you get away with that, you're as deranged as she is."

"It doesn't matter that she got inside my head. I'm still the one who... I drove a fucking stake through your chest, Jacinda. I very nearly ended your life."

He slid a hand beneath the hem of her blouse, his palm easing across her abdomen, fingers brushing the puckered scar where the stake and her sister's dark magic had done their nasty business.

"When someone hurts you," he said, "I feel this overwhelming need to make it right. Not just to hurt them back—to take them out of the fucking equation completely. But this time, the monster who hurt you—the monster who nearly killed you—was me. And I don't know what the fuck to do with that. How to make it right. How to..." His voice shattered, his anguish so dark and deep, she felt the echo of it in her own heart. "I'm sorry. I'm so sorry I hurt you, Jace. So sorry I didn't have the courage to say this sooner. I've been going out of my mind for days, trying to find a way to make it right, but I just don't know how."

"You're here," she said. "You showed up. That's all you ever had to do."

Gabriel closed his eyes and drew her closer, holding her tight, pressing a long, lingering kiss to the top of her head. His heart thrummed against her chest, making her feel more safe and protected and alive than she had in days.

In that moment, Jaci wanted nothing more than to close her eyes and let herself believe she'd finally found the fairy-tale, just like Charley and Dorian.

She knew now, despite everything they'd done to each other, Gabriel cared for her. Maybe even loved her, just as she loved him—recklessly and unapologetically. Effortlessly.

Maybe Charley had been right about that—about love being the easy part.

But that didn't mean they could overcome the rest. All that so-called messy, complicated shit was still a big tangled knot sitting between them. All the cruel things he'd said to her that first night in Bloodbath and in the early days that followed, all her lies about her demonic origins and Viansa's connection to the Redthorne curse, her plan to carve out his heart... All those past mistakes felt like their own kind of curse, woven so tightly and with so many different threads, Jaci didn't even know how to begin unraveling them. If it was even possible.

But for now, after far too long an absence, he was here. Maybe as a partner, maybe as a lover, maybe even as a friend. It didn't matter. Whatever Gabriel was, he *belonged* to her. Not in a possessive way—maybe not even in a romantic one. Just in the quiet way a person can slip into your heart and change the shape of it, forever becoming a part of you.

"Will you do something for me?" she asked softly.

"Name it," he whispered. "Whatever you need."

"I'm so glad you said that, Prince." A smile slid across Jaci's lips, and she stretched up onto her toes, whispering a single command in his ear. "Strip."

CHAPTER TWENTY-ONE

"What the bloody hell have I gotten myself into, woman?"

Perched on the edge of the bathroom vanity, Jaci laughed, enjoying the show. "For a two-hundred-fifty-something-year-old vampire, you sure know how to throw a temper tantrum. Seriously—you could do ten rounds with a toddler and come out on top every time."

"I told you, I don't favor baths. Especially solo baths. What's the bloody point?" Gabriel glared up at her from the tub, the steaming hot water lapping at his chest, translucent from the combination of magical ingredients she'd added— sea salt, honey, bay leaves, black pepper oil, white rose petals, and two fist-sized rose quartz crystals.

On the toiletry shelf above his head, a large white candle carved with protective runes burned bright, centered between two Tarot cards.

The Star was for healing, protection, and guidance, featuring a black-haired woman pouring out two grails of blood—one onto a bouquet of dried winter roses, the other onto a summer rosebush blooming with fresh flowers. Behind her, a cloaked woman stood sentry with a bright candle, ready to lead her back out through the darkened forest.

The Lord of Knives was the second card—a ghostly knight riding on a white horse, his black blade piercing the dark clouds that surrounded them, revealing the light. Jaci had selected that one for strength, clear vision, and frankly —a little extra ass-kickery.

She'd taken a similar ritual bath last night, but this was different. This was Gabriel, the vampire she'd longed for, the vampire who'd always protected her, whether he realized it or not.

And now he was here, naked, rock-hard from the moment she'd told him to strip, his muscled chest slick with water and heat. A thin trail of dark hair led down into the water—a path she desperately wanted to follow with her tongue. But that would make an even bigger mess of her makeup than her earlier tears, and she'd just finished reapplying everything.

"And I told *you*," she finally said, forcing her gaze back to his, "it's a protection ritual, and it's important to me. Now dunk."

Huffing out an exasperated breath, he slipped beneath the water, then popped back up, dark hair plastered to his head, a rose petal snagged in the stubble along his jaw.

He shoved the hair out of his eyes and resumed his glaring. "I hardly need protection. I'm an immortal vampire, for fuck's sake. You, on the other hand—"

"Humor me."

"If it's a good time you're after, witch, I can think of at least a dozen other things we can do in the bath."

"I'm sure you can."

He held out a hand, dripping water onto the floor. "Care to join me, little moonflower? You'll have to remove your clothing first, though. Water's no good for leather and silk, and neither are my teeth when I'm tearing my way through them."

He grinned and showed a flash of fang, the sight making her heart stutter.

The idea of Gabriel shredding her clothes with his teeth...

"Pass," she said firmly.

"You're certain?" he teased. "The water is perfect. Very, very hot. And very, very... wet."

"As bathwater tends to be."

"Could be hotter, though. With the right..." He licked his lower lip, letting his gaze roam down her body. "...approach."

The deep sultriness in his voice mingled with the hunger in his eyes and the steam from the bath, the whole combo making Jaci undeniably wet, weak in the knees, and *more* than ready to take him up on the offer. She could almost feel the slide of his strong, firm hands over her slippery flesh, the tangle of their legs beneath the surface, the press of his urgent mouth on her neck, on her nipple...

No, girl. Vlad the battery-powered Impaler is the only safe bet. We talked about this, remember?

Jaci closed her eyes, trying to calm the wild heartbeat she knew Gabriel could sense. As much as she'd love to give in to her obvious desire, her feelings for him—the real ones—were just too thorny. She had no idea whether he was merely interested in a good time—okay, fine, a monumentally, mind-blowingly *orgasmic* time—or something deeper, and right now, she couldn't risk either.

Everything between them was just too complicated, with way too much at stake.

Pun *not* intended.

Opening her eyes and focusing on a chipped tile just behind his shoulder, she said, "Here's how this works, Prince. You're either cooperating with me willingly, or I'm roasting your ass with hellfire and finishing the spell the hard way. Now dunk."

"Are you always so obstinate?"

"Only when I'm right."

"No. You're *always* obstinate."

"Exactly." She flashed a grin, then dropped it, scowling at him instead. "Dunk, Prince. This time, stay under for thirty seconds, and visualize yourself being enveloped in a bubble of pure white light."

"I hardly think—"

"Thirty seconds, white light, or we'll have to start all over again."

With a litany of whispered curses, he finally submerged

himself again, and Jaci returned to the mirror to touch up her hair.

Thirty seconds later, he breeched the surface like a whale, splashing half the water and rose petals onto the floor. "How much bloody good will all this white-light, protection-ritual mojo actually do against a succubus that can control minds and appear and disappear at will?"

"Only a little, but that's better than zilch, which is what you started with. Isabelle and I talked about warding Obsidian and the residences, but warding isn't specific enough. We'd have to ward against *all* demons, which would cut your clientele in half and leave me out on my ass as well."

"Yes, and what *about* you? Shouldn't you be in here with me? Where's your protection spell?"

"I did it last night."

"*Fuck*. If only I'd come sooner."

"That's what *she* said," she muttered.

"What?"

"I mean… I…" Jaci took a breath. Blew it out. Stopped thinking about Gabriel making her come. "I already did the protection ritual on myself, just as a precaution. But when it comes to Viansa, there's really only one thing that can protect me: taking that bitch down for good."

"I thought you said we couldn't kill her."

"No, I said we couldn't kill her *yet*." She plucked a smaller rose quartz crystal from the dish on the sink and chucked it into the bathwater, right between his legs. "Now dunk again.

And this time, I want you to stay under for as long as you can, keeping that protective bubble of light in your mind's eye until you feel it solidify around you like magical armor."

Gabriel shot her another glare. "Obstinate witch."

"Obstinate *demon* witch," she reminded him, calling a flame of hellfire to her fingertips. "Don't test me, Prince."

Gabriel grumbled, sighed, and scrubbed a hand over his face, then slipped below the water once more.

And Jaci, stifling a giggle, slipped out the door, grabbed her coat and purse, and headed off to Obsidian.

CHAPTER TWENTY-TWO

"You're hovering again, Prince."

"Yes, it's a thing I do now." Gabriel stepped behind his witch and rested his chin on her shoulder, trying to read the tiny print on the ancient occult tome she'd spread open on the bar. "*Hover*."

"Well stop. You're messing with my vibe." She slammed the book shut and tried to shrug him off, but there was no real force—not in her words, and certainly not in her meager efforts to escape.

"Should've considered that before your little bathtub prank, witch." He slid a hand across her stomach and nuzzled the back of her neck. Her hair was pulled into a loose bun, giving him clear access to her bare skin. To her intoxicating earth-and-pepper scent. "You won't be leaving my sights—or my hands—anytime soon."

"Worst punishment *ever*." She turned around in his arms and threaded her fingers into his hair, staring up at him with those fiery blue eyes. "Are you sure you don't want to lock me in the dungeon instead? Strip me down, chain me up, whip me into submission?"

"Mmm." Gabriel leaned in close and nipped her earlobe, his voice a dark whisper. "Don't push me, little moonflower."

When he looked at her again, she held his gaze for a long moment, a challenge flashing in hers, the warmth of her body conspiring with the softness of her mouth to make his cock throb with desperate, aching need.

Her effect on him was constant and obvious, and he saw it in her eyes the instant it registered now—pupils dilating, lids growing heavy.

"Gabriel," she breathed, closing her eyes and nibbling her lower lip, and he held his breath, heart pounding, wondering if this would be it—the moment they finally gave in to the pull.

But then she shook her head and turned away without another word, heading over to the cocktail table where she'd stacked the rest of Isabelle's books.

Gabriel let out a frustrated sigh.

He didn't blame her, though. Just as often, he'd been the one to turn away first.

Two weeks had passed since Viansa's attack, and that's just how it was now. A few flirty innuendos, a sensual touch that ended far too quickly. The night he'd visited her with the mint had certainly brought them closer—closer toward forgiveness, toward trust, toward admitting what they both so clearly felt. But with that new closeness had also come a new fear—the sharp and sudden realization of just how much power they had to hurt each other.

Gabriel glanced out across the bar, watching as Jacinda bent over another tome, frantically scribbling notes onto a yellow legal pad. His heart bled just to look at her—a clear reminder of its fragility in the face of something so immense. So unfamiliar.

That was the paradox of love.

The heart was a terrifying thing to risk, yet without that risk, one could never truly love. Could never *feel* it—feel it the way Gabriel felt it when he held her in his arms, when she brewed him another mug of tea or mixed another drink she thought he'd enjoy, when he watched her now, searching beneath her books for the pencil she'd stuck into the pile of curls on her head seconds earlier.

Gabriel crossed the room, plucked the pencil from her hair.

Jacinda laughed and said, "What would I do without you, Prince?"

Gabriel shrugged. "Guess we'll never know."

He winked, then headed back behind the bar, finishing up a liquor order he'd started earlier.

They spent most of their waking moments together at Obsidian now, Jacinda working on her research or working behind the bar, Gabriel managing the club and dealing with endless security meetings, conferences with Cole and his brothers, and regular visits from Isabelle, whose magical infusions he, Dorian, and Colin required more often now.

Late at night, after hours, Gabriel and Jacinda would

walk home together, always ending up at her place. He stayed with her now, holding her while they slept in her bed, his own too fraught with the memories of Viansa's first appearance. When the sun roused them from sleep, they'd make breakfast together, or occasionally pick something up from one of the many diners or delis in the neighborhood on their walk to Obsidian, then get back to work. The club. The search for Viansa. The search for the binding spell. The search for the cure.

It was a routine now—*their* routine—a thing that had snuck up on him, embedding itself in his life long before he recognized what was happening.

And now that he had, he didn't want to let it go.

"You're doing it again," Jacinda slammed another book shut and glanced up from her seat at the cocktail table, her eyes bleary, hair slipping from the bun.

"We both know you love it when I hover." Gabriel stepped behind her and grabbed her shoulders, massaging away the knots. "Now tell me what's really bothering you."

She rolled her neck, easing into his touch. "We've been at this for weeks. No clues in these books—at least, none that we've been able to put together. Cole hasn't figured out what's going on with Duchanes and the mages. And worse, there's been no sign of my sister since the big stake-and-run."

"She'll turn up, Jace. She didn't come all this way just to pack it in and go home."

"That's what I'm afraid of. Lying low? It's not her style, Prince. Viansa may have big plans, but she's not strategic—she's dramatic. Something major is brewing, and I'm worried none of us will see it coming. And this time, we might not be able to fix it."

Gabriel said nothing. She was right on all counts, and every last one of her worries was his as well.

Jacinda pushed her fingers into her hair and sighed, her head drooping low. "I'm starting to feel like the walls are closing in on me. I can't even remember the last time I felt actual dirt beneath my feet."

"Not a fan of concrete?" he teased. "We grow some of the very best of it here in New York."

"Yes, and the official state tree is the orange construction cone. Impressive." Jacinda laughed, but Gabriel heard the longing in her voice.

During his time in New York, then in Las Vegas, then back to New York again, Gabriel had all but forgotten what it was like to regularly walk on grass, to look up at night and see the stars, to hear the song of crickets or the howl of the winter wind absent the cacophony of urban existence.

Before Jacinda had come into his life, he'd been too focused on building his empire and outrunning his ghosts to really notice his bleak environment, much less care about his severed connection from the natural world.

But Jacinda cared. She was an earth witch. She thrived

on that connection—needed it, perhaps now more than ever.

"I want you to do three things for me," he said suddenly. "Put all this stuff away, call Maritza and tell her she's in charge here tonight, and meet me back here in fifteen minutes."

"But... Why?" She tilted her head back and narrowed her eyes, new light sparkling through their blue depths. "What are you plotting, Prince?"

Gabriel leaned in close, kissing the shell of her ear.

"Something dirty," he whispered. "Something *very* dirty."

CHAPTER TWENTY-THREE

Nearly two hundred years had passed since Gabriel last visited the Enchanted Gardens, and the sight still had the power to steal his breath.

Tucked away in a hidden corner of the Bronx, the indoor park had been vast and beautiful in his memory, but now— seeing it through Jacinda's eyes—it felt even grander, with hundreds of criss-crossing dirt pathways that wound through an arboretum, a bird sanctuary, and flowering gardens exploding with colorful blooms, all of it immune to winter's icy touch.

Tonight, at Gabriel's request—and with a sizable transfer of funds no man could refuse—the park had been closed to the public.

"What is this place?" Jacinda whispered, wonder shining in her eyes as he escorted her to the rosebushes— the area he knew she'd most love.

Fairy lights and paper lanterns illuminated the

Enchanted Gardens, lending credence to its name and making him feel as if they'd stepped into another world. Even just a few dozen feet beyond the entrance, the sensory assault of the city had already faded. The temperature was warm and comfortable, the air scented with flowers, the occasional flapping of a bird's wings their only company.

"The Rothsman Enchanted Gardens," Gabriel said, draping their winter coats across a park bench.

He was still dressed in the black suit he'd put on earlier for work, but now he ditched the tie, abandoning it with their coats. Jacinda wore a fitted button-down sweater and a pair of dark jeans that hugged her arse, the combination making him itch to run his hands along every curve.

"Here?" she asked, as if she still couldn't believe it. "In New York City?"

"It's a little-known secret, nearly forgotten among the splashier tourist attractions. It's been here since the mid-1800s, maintained by the same family—humans, if you can believe it. Passed on from one generation to the next. My brothers and I attended the grand opening."

"Wow. That must've been incredible."

"It was a different time, to be sure. The city was still bustling with life—just not in quite the same way it is today."

"I'm glad no one else knows about this place now. It's like a little slice of untouched heaven in the midst of concrete hell."

"And not an orange cone in sight." Grinning, Gabriel

put an arm around her shoulders and pulled her close. "Shall we wander?"

"I'd love to, but…" She glanced behind them, then back to Gabriel, lowering her voice as if they were about to plan a felony. "It's closed for a private event. There was a sign out front—"

"Placed there at my request."

"Really?" She smiled so earnestly, it made Gabriel's heart skip.

"Really. Now let's go, before the clock strikes midnight and our coach turns back into a pumpkin."

The rose gardens were breathtaking—rows upon rows of blooms so deeply red they were almost black, gradually transforming to lighter reds and pinks as they continued along the path. In every direction, new pathways branched off, boasting even more colors—creams and yellows, oranges, violets. It was as if the whole place had been carpeted in a living rainbow, and the more time they spent among the rosebushes, the more lively Jacinda became, her eyes brighter than they'd been in weeks, her cheeks flush with a joy that was as childlike as it was contagious.

In what looked to be the very center of the rose gardens, Jacinda slid out of her boots and socks and dug her toes into the damp earth, closing her eyes and letting out a contented sigh Gabriel couldn't help but mirror.

She was truly in her element, and he cursed himself for not bringing her here sooner.

Watching in quiet admiration as she soaked up the moment, he marveled once again at her beauty, her aliveness. But after a few blissful minutes, Jacinda's brow furrowed, and she gasped, turning and heading off down one of the paths, her steps urgent.

"What is it?" Gabriel asked, jogging to keep up.

They reached the end of the section with the white and cream-colored roses, and the last two bushes looked a little frail. Some of the blooms had already died, their petals brown and desiccated.

Wordlessly she knelt down in the dirt, cupping one of the dead blooms in her hands. She bent over it as a mother might a child, whispering an enchantment Gabriel couldn't hear.

Seconds later, the petals unfurled, the brown fading away as the original creamy-white returned.

Gabriel watched in amazement as she performed the same ritual on every dead bloom until the bushes were once again bursting with gloriously healthy roses.

Jacinda turned and looked up at him over her shoulder, beaming with pride and happiness.

"You brought them back to life," he whispered. "But that's…"

He didn't even have the word for it. Impossible? Miraculous?

"The roses weren't technically dead. Only a little sad." She ran her fingertips over one of the newly restored blooms. "Sometimes they get lonely at the end of the row here."

"The roses… They told you this?"

"Not with words, no. Plants have a language all their

own. Much more subtle than the spoken word, but just as complex and nuanced."

"You speak plant?"

"That's an interesting way of putting it, but yes. It's how I ask permission to work with them—everything from my teas to my Obsidian cocktails, my bath rituals, my cooking... Absolutely I speak to them. More importantly, I listen."

Gabriel stared at her open-mouthed, shock and awe warring for dominance inside him.

It was still so hard to reconcile. How could this sweet, incredible woman who brought so much life and beauty to the world be the same woman who'd resurrected the grays? Who'd been born in hell to a vicious demon? Who'd planned, however briefly, to kill him?

How could so much darkness thrive in a heart that shone with so much light?

Jacinda got to her feet and glanced at her palms, slowly rubbing at the dirt that'd gathered in the creases. Not to clear it away like most people would, but simply to feel it against her skin. To listen to it, perhaps, just as she'd listened to the lonely roses.

She closed her fingers over her palms and smiled, her eyes luminescent beneath the fairy lights. "Thank you for bringing me here. I really missed playing in the dirt."

He took in the sight of her—the full spectacle of it— three white rose petals stuck in her hair, her bright eyes shining, dirt caked under her fingernails, more of it blackening her jeans and her bare toes—and a feeling welled up inside him with the force of a volcano, hot and explosive and ready to erupt.

"Jacinda, I... I need to tell you something. It's important."

"You okay, Prince?" She looped her arms around his neck and leaned in close, and Gabriel breathed her in again, her familiar scent nearly overpowered by the roses that surrounded them.

Cradling her face in his hands, he said, "The first night we were... together. Physically. Do you remember?"

She laughed, her eyes twinkling. "The night you spied on me like a perv through your cameras, then charged into my bedroom and ravaged me?"

"Ravaged, plundered, devoured, all of the above." His cock stiffened at the memory, and he lowered his mouth to the hollow of her throat, dusting it with a soft kiss, then another, slowly working his way up to her ear. "You asked me if I remembered you from the Ravenswood fundraiser."

Jacinda shivered at his every word. His every feather-light kiss. "You said you didn't."

"No, little moonflower. I merely asked if I *should*." He dragged his lips along her jaw to her face, kissing one corner of her mouth, then the other, hovering close enough to taste her breath—cloves and cinnamon, a sweet and spicy mix that always drove him wild.

"Jacinda," he said softly, his voice as ragged as his heartbeat, "from the first moment I saw you in my brother's gardens, you've entranced me. *Nothing* could've chased you from my thoughts. By day, I saw you in the face of every passing stranger on the street, and when darkness fell, I saw you in the light of every rising moon. I saw you in my dreams. In my shadows. Everywhere I looked, there you were. There you *are*. Haunting me still."

Her eyes glazed with emotion, lips parting in silent surprise.

"I've tried a thousand different ways to not feel the things I feel for you," he whispered. "To recall every terrible thing we've ever said to each other, to list all the reasons this can't work, to give myself one more excuse to walk away. I've tried to forget you—begged the gods and the devil both to scrub you from my memories."

A tear slipped down her cheek, her eyes searching his in the soft light. "If you wanted to forget me so badly, why are you still here? Why are you even telling me all this?"

"Because somewhere between those dark, stolen moments at Ravenswood and the first time I held you close enough to see the fire in your eyes... Somewhere between watching you mix your first cocktail behind the bar and watching you dive in front of a stake to protect Charlotte... Somewhere between picking you up off the pavement after you wasted those grays near the hospital and tonight, witnessing the miracle of you whispering roses back to life... I fell in love with you, Jacinda Colburn. Madly, terrifyingly, obsessively in love with you. You asked if I *remembered* you? Bloody hell, woman, you took up so much room in my head, I could scarcely remember anything else. And now you've so thoroughly invaded my heart, I'm afraid it won't remember how to beat if I have to go another moment without kissing you."

She blinked once, twice, then she closed her eyes and took a deep breath, her body quaking in his embrace.

But in the wake of his most terrifying confession, the woman said nothing.

She was silent for so long, Gabriel began to wonder if he'd only said it in his mind.

If she'd gone into a trance partway through.

If she was still listening to the roses, his spoken English words falling on deaf ears.

Not long ago, Jacinda had talked about carving out his heart, but in that moment, Gabriel felt as if he'd done it for her, handing it over on a silver platter in an offering she'd yet to accept.

He waited.

And he waited.

And he fucking *waited*, and it felt as if the night bled into the day and back to night again, and still, his woman hadn't spoken.

"Jacinda," he whispered, and she finally opened her eyes.

"All right, Prince," she said, the sound of her voice nearly sending him to his knees. "You've said your piece. And now I've got something to say too."

"Tell me," he demanded, and there beneath the warm glow of the fairy lights, a smile broke across her beautiful face.

In that smile, Gabriel saw the rest of his immortal life. He saw his heart. He saw his home.

"Kiss me, Gabriel Redthorne," she said. "And don't you *dare* stop."

He didn't need any more words after that—English, plant, or otherwise.

He fisted her hair with both hands, his mouth crashing into hers like a wave breaking over the shore, washing away all the worry and fear, all the terrible mistakes of the past, everything but *this* moment, his woman melting in his arms, her soft moans filling his mouth, his hands tangling in her wild curls.

The kiss was breathtaking and epic, the kind of kiss that could start a war and end it just as easily, but it wasn't enough.

Gabriel needed more of her.

All of her.

He shrugged out of his suit jacket and tossed it into the dirt between the two rose bushes, then kissed his way down her throat, her chest, unbuttoning her sweater and blazing a hot trail between her breasts. He dropped to his knees, kissing the pink starburst scar of her wound, kissing her taut stomach, kissing her everywhere as his fingers unbuttoned, unzipped, and tugged.

Stepping out of her jeans and panties, Jacinda tried to hold on to his shoulders for balance, but in a swift move he swept her legs out from under her and caught her, gently laying her on his jacket. He kissed her mouth once more, then gripped her thighs, lowering his mouth to the hot, sweet flesh between them.

The scent of her desire hit him full on, making him dizzy.

He descended in a frenzy, circling her clit with his tongue, fast, then slow, dragging his mouth lower, licking and sucking as she knotted her fingers in his hair and arched to get closer.

"Gabriel," she breathed, and he remembered that night on the beach when they'd argued and she'd first called him by his given name. He'd hated the sound of it then, but now it was a symphony that made him hard and hungry and desperate for more. He moaned against her flesh, his tongue lashing her clit, then slipping inside, hands tightening around her thighs as he fucked her with his eager mouth, deeper and faster, pushing her harder, closer…

Her thighs trembled beneath his grip, hips rocking, blood rushing through her veins as the orgasm steadily built inside her…

Gabriel couldn't wait another moment. He needed to make her shatter, to taste her, to reclaim her from the brutal death that'd nearly stolen her two weeks back. A violent growl tore through his chest at the memory, and he thrust deep inside, taking her, marking her, fucking her until she came so hard on his tongue the earth rumbled and the trees quaked and a dozen white rose petals alighted on her bare thighs like the softest rain.

The taste of her was everything, and Gabriel would've gladly lingered, his tongue already drawing another lazy circle around her clit, certain he could make her come again. But the tug on his hair grew insistent, demanding, and when he finally glanced up, the look in his witch's eyes was so fierce, he knew she wanted something much more than his mouth.

He also knew that whatever it was, he wouldn't refuse.

"I want you to bite me," she finally said, fire smoldering in her gaze. "I want you to feed."

CHAPTER TWENTY-FOUR

I want you to feed.

The words echoed through Gabriel's mind, setting his skin on fire. His fangs sliced through his gums, mouth already watering for a taste of her exquisite blood. The scent of it alone was enough to drive him to the edge, but actually feeding on her... *Fuck.* That was a pleasure he'd only ever dreamed about.

Running a hand up her inner thigh, feeling the inviting pulse of her femoral artery, Gabriel drew in a deep breath. He thought to warn her. Thought to flat-out deny her request, even after swearing to himself that he wouldn't.

But when he looked into her eyes again, the ferocity he found there turned his hunger into a burning, fiery ache unmatched by any he'd ever felt before.

"Please," she begged. "Don't stop."

That was all he needed to hear.

He sank his fangs deep into her thigh, then closed his

lips around the wound and sucked, his tongue soothing the sting as she gasped and writhed beneath him.

"Holy fuck," she breathed. "Gabriel, that's…"

Yes, he knew *exactly* what it was. Despite the initial pain, the erotic euphoria of a vampire bite was legendary, and within seconds her heart was racing again, heat gathering between her thighs, her hips arching as she pressed herself harder against his insistent mouth.

Blood slid across his tongue, warm and sweet and devastating, his mind and body spinning with all the new sensations she unleashed inside him. The taste was indescribable—not the coppery blood of a witch, not the acrid blood of a demon, not even a blend of the two. Just a unique, intoxicating flavor all her own.

He filled his mouth, savoring every drop of her precious blood. There was an edge to it, a black smoke that made his heart beat faster, his skin tingle, his breath catch.

His cock rock fucking hard.

She tasted like sin and fire, like every dark thing he'd tried so foolishly to outrun when all along the darkness was the very thing keeping him alive.

He slid his hands around the backs of her thighs and brought her closer, drinking her, sucking. She gasped again, frantically tugging his hair, and he slid his mouth to her center, dragging his tongue through her wet heat, then back again, lapping up the blood that spilled across her skin.

Jacinda hadn't yet come a second time before she'd demanded the bite, and now he took pleasure in making her wait, drawing out her release as he took his fill, sucking here, licking there, teasing her with soft strokes of his tongue until he knew she couldn't take another moment of his torture.

Swallowing the last bit of blood he dared to take, Gabriel returned his attention to her clit, sucking it between his lips, flicking her with his tongue until she clamped her thighs tight around his head and cried out, tugging his hair so hard it made his eyes water.

When he finally pulled back, both of them were breathless. Panting.

A blush swept across Jacinda's cheeks and throat, a dark contrast to the white rose petals that haloed her silver hair.

The sweet fire of her blood sang through Gabriel's body, electric and pulsing and hot.

Magic.

He felt strong. Fucking *alive*, as if she'd just awoken him from a grave he hadn't even realized he'd fallen into.

A deep, possessive rumble vibrated through his chest. She belonged to him, only and always, and he needed to fuck her.

Now.

Without another thought he flipped her onto her stomach, hauling her hips up until she was on her hands and knees, half perched on his jacket, half in the dirt, her lush backside bared for her vampire prince. With a gentle touch that belied his desperation, he palmed her arse.

Jacinda arched her back and moaned in pleasure, a soft, decadent sound that stirred a deep ache in his balls.

"Fuck," he whispered. He closed his eyes, focusing entirely on the heat of her skin against his palm. "*Fuck.*"

With his other hand he freed his cock and moved closer to her, sliding along her entrance, making her shudder with every stroke.

"Don't stop," she begged again. "Please, Gabriel. I need you inside me. I feel like I'm on *fire.*"

The longing in her voice matched the ache in his chest. In his balls.

He fisted her long hair, winding it tight around his hand. With the very last breath in his lungs, he whispered, "I won't stop, little moonflower. I promise."

Gabriel took her right there. Down in the dirt between the rosebushes, her pale fingers clawing at the damp earth, thorns scratching her arms. He pulled her hair and forced her head back as he slammed into her again, hard and deep, a collision that unleashed a shock of desire so fierce it was like a living thing itself, a force the enchanting witch had resurrected just as she'd resurrected the flowers, with no more than her touch and a warm, heady breath.

He filled her completely, one hand gripping her hip, the silk of her hair twined in his fingers as he fucked her beneath the tangle of blooms and thorns, beauty and pain, the air thick with the scent of blood and roses and sex. She pushed back, meeting every thrust, taking him deeper, grinding against him until they reached the very edge of the cliff together.

This time, he issued no commands. Made no claims but the promise of his fevered touch.

Still fisting her hair, he plunged inside her one last time, blissfully erupting in an explosion of pure, white-hot ecstasy, and when she came for him, she cried out and shuddered around him, a full-bodied tremor that reverberated into his very bones, marking him as deeply as he'd marked her.

Mine.

When the breath finally returned to his lungs, Gabriel slid out from inside her, and Jacinda turned over and stretched out on her back, her eyes closed, a smile touching her lips. He collapsed on top of her and held her close, nuzzling her neck, breathing her in, listening to the rhythmic beat of her heart. The taste of her lingered in his mouth—blood and desire both—and Gabriel closed his eyes and sighed, remembering the Tarot card that'd slipped from her deck the night she'd told him about its messages.

A vampire embracing his woman on a bed of roses.

The Lovers.

That night, he'd asked her if she believed love was a choice.

Now, holding her beneath the rosebushes, he knew the truth of it.

Love wasn't a choice at all.

The choice was what came after. What did we do with such a precious gift? Did we cherish and nurture it, encouraging its gentle bloom? Or did we smother or neglect it until it withered and died on the vine?

Gabriel had already made his choice.

The next belonged to her.

Slowly, he got to his feet and put himself back together, then held out his hand—an offer. A plea.

And Jacinda—his beautiful, fiery, dark, light, magical, mysterious witch-demon—laughed and reached for him and grabbed on tight.

CHAPTER TWENTY-FIVE

Long after Jaci and her vampire prince returned to the high-way, the scent of roses still lingered, along with the sizzling heat in all the places he'd touched her and the echo of the words that'd sent her heart soaring.

I fell in love with you, Jacinda Colburn...

Now, with every beat of that soaring heart, the erotic ache of Gabriel's bite throbbed anew, a seductive reminder of all the things they'd shared tonight in the Gardens.

No matter what the future held for them, Jaci knew this was one of those nights that would mark her forever, dividing her life into all its befores and afters, every last one of them pivoting around *this* moment. *This* feeling.

Madly, terrifyingly, obsessively in love with you...

Suddenly, Gabriel slowed the car and took an unfamiliar exit, pulling her from her reverie.

"What's going on?" she asked, shattering the comfortable silence that'd fallen between them. "This isn't the way back to the city."

Gabriel grinned at her across the dark space of the car. "We're not going back to the city. Not until tomorrow, anyway. And before you say a word, I've already checked in with Dorian and Aiden—they've got everything under control. The club, the security, the endless search for the bitch I refuse to name tonight—it's all being handled. I spoke with Cole as well—he's got some of his wolves with him on the Jersey stakeout, hoping to cover a bit more ground. Oh, and Charlotte says hello, and something about an upcoming Fifty Shades movie marathon and hot tub party at Ravenswood with her and Sasha? I didn't press for details, but she was quite adamant I relay the message, and quite adamant the invitation did *not* extend to me and Dorian."

"But..." Jaci blinked, trying to adjust to the rapid-fire change of plans. Her first instinct was to demand he take her back home—that they'd already had their fun tonight and couldn't spare any more time away from their work. The binding spell, the bitch-who-shall-not-be-named, Jaci's endlessly failing attempts to connect with Meech... There was still so much to do. To figure out.

But then he slipped a hand behind her neck and squeezed, and all the tension melted away in an instant.

"Okay, you win," she finally said. "One night to forget about everything else. Just one, then it's back to reality."

"I'm so relieved to hear you say that. After what I put

him through to get things ready for us, my associate would decapitate me if I canceled now."

"Things? What things? And what associate?" Jaci laughed. "Where are you taking me? Nowhere public, I hope. I'm filthy, Gabriel!"

"Which, coincidentally, is exactly how I like you."

"*Location*, Prince. Spill it."

"It's a surprise."

"Two in one night?"

He arched an eyebrow, sexy as ever. "I'm just getting started, little moonflower."

Giddiness bubbled up inside, making her feel light and airy in a way she hadn't since she was a kid. And even back then, those fizzy kinds of moments were few and far between: sneaking into her mother's private quarters with Meech, stealing bottles from her collection of ancient magical elixirs. Her father, taking her to see the triple suns rise over the black ocean in hell's Vargas realm—by night, the waters turned to acid, the beach crawling with horrifying beasts with daggers for teeth and claws that could shred an elephant, but the rising dawn was one of the most amazing things she'd ever seen. Another time, her father had shown her how to find water beneath the parched earth of the Salt Flats. And on her tenth birthday, after a particularly brutal fight with Viansa that'd left Jaci with a broken arm and three missing teeth, he'd given her a bouquet of stargazer lilies that sparkled like real stars.

He'd bred and grown them himself, all from different botanicals he'd gathered across the realms.

Even in hell, there was beauty to be found, just like finding an enchanted oasis in the middle of a concrete jungle.

"What are you thinking about?" Gabriel brushed his knuckles along her jaw. "You're smiling."

Jaci let out a soft sigh. "My dad, actually. He'd really love the Enchanted Gardens. He's an earth mage, too." She told him about the lilies.

"Now I know where you get your gifts." Gabriel lowered his hand to her knee, giving it a squeeze. "When this is all over, we'll have to take him to the Gardens."

The idea filled her with hope, but she knew better than to hold onto it too tightly. "Gabriel, I don't... I'm not even sure if he's still—"

"He is. I promise you."

"I appreciate the optimism, but you can't know that. I haven't seen him in a month. Haven't made a single payment since then, either. For all I know, he's out on the street by now. Or worse."

"Jacinda..." Gabriel turned to look at her again, his green eyes briefly illuminated by a streetlight they'd just passed. "Colin and I... After you told me about Zachary's situation, I asked Colin to look in on him. Just once—we didn't want to risk alerting Viansa—but I wanted to be sure he was receiving the best possible care. Colin assured me the staff is top-notch, and aside from the supernatural issue, his condition was stable, all things considered. You don't need to worry about the bills, either—it's all been taken care of."

"You... really?" Her throat tightened, tears stinging the backs of her eyes. "You did all that... for me? Even after everything?"

Gabriel didn't respond.

"I thought you wanted to kill me that day," she whispered. "I honestly thought we'd never get close and—"

"I said a lot of terrible things that day." Gabriel tightened his grip on her knee. "I was angry and hurt and *supremely* fucked in the head, and if I could erase those words from your memory as well as my own, I would."

"It's not like I didn't earn them."

"Jacinda," he breathed, shaking his head, but whatever he'd meant to say next, it never came.

Jaci didn't push. Just took his hand in hers, lacing their fingers together as they continued down a snowy, treelined road, as far from civilization as she'd ever been in this realm.

Silence fell between them once more, but it wasn't the silent tension of an ongoing argument, of dark secrets coming to light, of lies and terrors and all the big and tiny things that drove people apart. This kind of silence felt like a new place, one she'd never visited before. A place where hope and possibility grew from the ashes of a ruined past finally buried.

"We're here," he said, turning onto a long driveway that snaked deeper into the woods. Snow blanketed the evergreens that surrounded them, but the driveway itself had been recently plowed. As they continued to thread their way through the trees, a two-story A-frame cabin slowly came into view, with massive windows that spilled warm, inviting light into the darkness. Smoke drifted lazily from a chimney on the rooftop, the scent of firewood making her feel cozy inside, despite the frigid winter night.

Gabriel parked the car in the small detached garage, then came around to open the passenger door for her. Beaming at him, Jaci threw herself into his embrace, unable to stop the giggle that burst free from inside.

"What have you done, Prince?" she teased.

"Made a few calls, is all."

"And?"

"And let's go find out, shall we?" Gabriel retrieved an overnight bag from the trunk—one she hadn't even known he'd packed—and took her hand, leading her along a recently shoveled path from the garage to the front porch.

It was beautiful, the whole world utterly silent save for the sound of their footsteps.

When they reached the porch and stopped to take it all in, the silence of the night enveloped them completely. It was so quiet Jaci heard the treetops whispering, their snowy blankets shifting on their shoulders.

"Stay here a moment," Gabriel said. "Enjoy the fresh air. I'll be right back."

He headed inside with the bag. A few minutes later, all the lights went out inside the cabin, bathing her in all-consuming darkness.

She was about to call out for him when he appeared at her side. He pressed a powder-soft kiss to her lips, then handed her a glass of red wine, tucking her under his arm.

"What's all this?" she asked.

"This," he said, holding up his own glass, "is an extremely rare Bordeaux. The very last bottle in existence, as a matter of fact, since you smashed the other one to bits."

"What?" She cracked up, remembering that day in the Obsidian wine cellar. "That's on you, Prince. If you hadn't manhandled me—"

"Manhandled? I was merely teaching you a lesson about the consequences of walking away from me in the middle of a conversation."

"Oh, is that what we were doing? Having a conversation?"

"Mmm. I *do* love conversing with you. You're an *excellent* conversationalist. Especially when you're wearing that little black thong and my fingers are buried in your hot, wet pussy, desperate to make you come." Gabriel leaned in and kissed her jaw, a soft moan vibrating from his lips, his cock pressing hard against her hip. "I packed the thong in the bag, you know. Just in case you want to have another… conversation."

"As much as I'd love to *converse* with that dirty mouth of yours," she teased, gently pushing him away, "it'll have to wait. Now that you've made such a production over it, I *really* need to taste this wine."

She brought the glass to her lips, but he stopped her before she could take the first sip, his eyes turning serious.

"When was the last time you've seen the stars?" he asked softly.

"Honestly, I'm not sure." Jaci shrugged. "The city lights

always drown them out. I feel them, though. Their presence. Their magic."

"Tonight you get to look at them, too." He tilted his head back, and she did the same, taking in the view of the sky for the first time since they'd arrived.

Jaci gasped, her heart fluttering in her chest, her eyes watering at the impossible vastness of it.

The Milky Way splashed across the sky as if it'd been spilled from a giant bucket, every star glittering like ice in a vast sea of darkness.

She'd never seen anything like it. Not even the triple suns glinting off the black ocean could compare.

"It's almost unfair that something can be so beautiful," she whispered, a tear sliding down her cheek.

"It's bloody heartbreaking," he murmured, but when Jaci lowered her gaze, she found Gabriel wasn't looking at the star-swept sky at all.

He was looking at her.

"Happy Solstice, Jacinda." He touched his glass to hers, his tone soft and somber. "I won't pretend to know much about it from a magical perspective, but I do know it's the longest, darkest night of the year, and after seeing you cooped up for so long with the books and the stress and... I don't know. I thought maybe, just for tonight, we could go somewhere where we could appreciate it."

"It's perfect, Prince. Happy Solstice."

They sipped the wine, Gabriel clearly enjoying the taste, Jaci trying to hide the fact that she was about to cry. And laugh. And cry all over again. Her emotions were a rollercoaster tonight—all because an infuriating, commanding, impossibly sexy vampire had the audacity to fall in love with her.

"Thank you," she finally managed. "I don't think I even realized how badly I needed this."

"The wine?"

"The darkness," she whispered, as if the word itself were sacred tonight.

Gabriel's smile faded, and he nodded, brushing his thumb across her lips. "I think maybe I needed the darkness too."

They finished their wine in silence, gazing up at the stars until Jaci's feet turned numb and the clouds swept through the sky, ushering in a cold wind and the first few snowflakes that foretold of the coming storm.

Outside their cozy cabin, the blizzard raged, lashing the windows with heavy, wet snow that quickly turned to ice.

But inside, encased in their own little snow-globe world, the vampire prince unleashed a different kind of storm.

Starting in the shower, where they took their time scrubbing each other clean of the the dirt and renegade rose petals, exploring every slippery curve—first with soap and water, then with hands and mouths.

Later, they moved on to the living room, where they stretched out naked on the bearskin rug before the fireplace, alternating between long, lingering caresses and the feral, devastating intensity Gabriel seemed to love most of all.

Jaci loved it too, her body electrified by his every touch —his hot mouth on her nipple, teeth scraping her sensitive flesh. His dark head between her thighs, devouring her with his tongue. His strong hands pinning her down as he plunged inside, fucking her until her shoulders burned raw from the rug, and the stars she'd seen in the night sky appeared behind her eyes.

She was driving him just as wild, dropping to her knees before him, worshipping his smooth, perfect cock with her mouth while he fisted her hair, desperate to hold on to his control as she stole it away from him one delicious stroke at a time. There were few things she enjoyed more than seeing the primal hunger in his eyes while he watched her sucking him, more than hearing the growl in his throat when he finally gave up that control, his body trembling as he came undone.

For her. *Because* of her.

Gabriel made her dizzy and happy and gloriously, fiendishly horny, and for the first time in her seven years in this realm—tonight, on the longest, darkest of nights—she almost forgot about all the things she'd left, however temporarily, behind.

But later, as she snuggled into the embrace of the vampire she loved, their bodies exquisitely spent, the fire no more than glowing embers before them, the universe decided to remind her.

No matter how many roses bloomed at your touch, no

matter how far out in the middle of nowhere you hid, no matter how perfectly the ice encased you in your pristine, snow-globe little world, the ghosts of the past would *always* hunt you down.

And they would *always* make you pay.

CHAPTER TWENTY-SIX

The darkness made anything seem possible.

And in that darkness, for the first time in his unnaturally long existence, Gabriel allowed himself to believe that maybe—just maybe—this could be his life.

She could be his life.

He lay on the bearskin rug beneath a down comforter, the woman he loved wrapped around him in a tangle of limbs and long silver curls and soft, contented sighs that caressed his bare chest. His body was exhausted from all the things they'd done to each other, but already, he couldn't wait to do them again. If she wasn't sleeping so peacefully beside him, he'd have her on all fours, her hair wrapped around his fist...

That's all it took. He was fucking hard for her again.

And with the image of her perfect arse in his mind, he finally drifted off to sleep.

"Wake up," she whispered against the back of his neck, making the fine hairs stand on end. "You have a visitor, sweetness. Wake up."

Gabriel sat up with a start, shocked to find he was alone at Obsidian again, hunched over the bar and nursing a bottle of bourbon. He could've sworn something had disturbed him—a whisper? A woman?—but when he glanced around, he saw no one.

He tipped the bottle against his lips, but it wasn't his beloved bourbon. Not anymore.

Ash coated his mouth, and a deep cough rattled through his chest. He spit it out violently, wet, black ash splattering across the bar.

From the furthest recesses of his mind, something stirred to life. A voice he couldn't understand. A gnawing persistence that felt like a warning, but...

The doors to Obsidian blew open, and a woman entered on a cold, acrid breeze. Behind her, St. Mark's Place was a wasteland, as if the entire city had been leveled by a volcano. A bomb.

Hellfire.

When had it happened? He couldn't recall. Just knew that it *had* happened.

"We're closed," he said, but the woman wasn't deterred. She took the barstool next to him, shaking out long hair the color of a raven's wing.

"Do I... Do I know you?" he asked, scrutinizing her face.

"I'm quite sure you do, sweetness." She flashed a blood-red smile, then leaned in to kiss him.

The instant her lips touched his, a blinding pain split Gabriel's skull, shattering something inside. It felt as if a dam had broken, all the old memories flooding into his awareness.

He'd been here before. This moment, this scene.

It wasn't real.

It was a dream. A nightmare.

The succubus was trying to control him again.

"You can't hide from me," she said, stroking his face. "Not for long."

"Get out of my fucking head!" he roared, shoving her away. She vanished in a cloud of black smoke, and when Gabriel turned back around, he found Jacinda behind the bar, her eyes full of terror.

Two demons crowded around her.

He remembered this moment, too. Kostya and He Who Likes to Watch.

Kostya ran his hand down her curves. "You have missed me, butterfly."

Dream or not, Gabriel blurred into them, taking down both demons in a flash of torn throats and severed limbs. They fell at his feet, blood spilling across the floor.

"Why would you do that?" Jacinda asked, her voice pained. When Gabriel looked up, he saw that he'd taken out her heart by mistake. It pulsed in his hand, warm and wet.

"No!" He tried frantically to put her back together, to heal her, but he couldn't. There were too many people in the way now, a dozen new figures emerging from the shadows, circling her, blocking her from Gabriel's reach. Tall mages in dark robes, chanting in a language whose words he didn't recognize. He slammed his fist through the back of the closest one, ripping out his spine. When the body dropped, Gabriel saw the gray-eyed mage with one hand in Jacinda's hair, his silver blade pressed to her throat.

The mage met his eyes. Grinned wickedly. And sliced.

Gabriel reached for her, catching her as she fell forward in a spray of blood. He gathered her against his chest, but they were no longer at the bar.

They were on the beach, running from an angry sea. Too slow. Too heavy. The wave caught them hard, knocking them down and sweeping them under, churning and churning until it finally spat them out.

They were back at Obsidian.

Now she stood before Charley, holding out her hands as if to stop Gabriel's advance. But Gabriel didn't want to stop. He shoved the stake into her chest. Blood coated his hands, and as she watched in horror, he licked them clean.

"I hate you, Prince," she whispered.

The words shook something loose inside.

"Jacinda?" He reached for her again, but it was too late.

Flames gathered at her feet, rising higher, burning them both. Now, she was in hell, chained to a jagged black rock that jutted up from a desolate landscape. Gabriel wanted desperately to free her, but every time he reached for the chains, the fire surged, melting his flesh. His bones.

"I can't save you!" he shouted. "I can't bloody save you!"

Jacinda laughed. "I told you, Prince. I'm not your damsel."

And then, shaking free of her chains, she stepped out of the fire, lifted her hands, and roasted him alive.

"No!" Gabriel bolted upright, still trapped in the midst of his delirium. Before him, the embers of the fire glowed, and he reached for them, so certain it was Jacinda, that she was burning, that he was losing her...

The heat of the embers shocked him fully awake, and he gasped, his body covered in sweat, every part of him trembling.

Jacinda stirred on the rug beside him, burrowing deeper beneath the comforter.

Relief flooded his chest.

He reached for her, shifting the bedding so he could touch her silver hair.

But it wasn't silver. It was black.

"I don't know what she did to you," the succubus hissed, "but you can't keep running forever, sweetness. I'll—"

Her image flickered, and the woman at his side became Jacinda once more.

Gabriel jammed the heels of his hands into his eyes, trying to get a fucking grip.

"Jacinda," he called out. "Wake up. *Please* wake up."

No response.

When he lowered his hands and opened his eyes, there was no Jacinda. No succubus. Nothing but a trail of fresh blood leading out through the front door.

He followed it outside, wading into knee-deep snow, ignoring the icy burn on his bare flesh. The blood carved a ruby-red path through the pristine whiteness, ending just before a copse of evergreens a few dozen yards out.

When he reached the trees, another figure stepped out from the shadows.

Gabriel fell to his knees and wept.

Between two pine trees, the child who'd haunted him his entire immortal life stood before him, her vacant eyes boring right into his soul.

The blood on her dress was bright red now, and she held something behind her back, intentionally hiding it from him. Blood dripped onto the snow behind her, sizzling.

She took a step toward him. Then another.

The change in her routine was alarming, but Gabriel didn't move. Didn't breathe.

The child leaned close, her breath sour. "Wake up, vampire prince. There's a wolf at the door."

~

"Fuck!" He bolted up from the floor and shot to his feet, gulping in air and desperately rubbing the chill from his arms.

He was back inside, the embers still glowing. No blood on the floor. No succubus. Nothing but his woman, sitting up and clutching the comforter to her chest, slowly blinking away the confusion of sleep.

"Gabriel? What's wrong?" She got to her feet. Reached for his arm. "You're trembling."

Behind her, the child flickered back into view.

Gabriel closed his eyes. Took another deep, steadying breath. Opened them again. Focused on Jacinda's blue eyes. On the wrinkle of concern between her eyebrows. On the silver-blond curl that fell over her forehead.

"It's really you," he whispered, and she smiled.

"Bad dreams?"

"I think I just…"

Behind her, the child shifted back into view. Unwavering. Bloody. Vacant.

"Gabriel, what are you looking at? What's wrong?" Jacinda turned to follow the line of his gaze, and for a moment he wished she'd see the child too. That he wasn't going fucking crazy.

"Do you see her?" he whispered.

"Who?" Jacinda looked back at him, her eyes narrowed. "Gabriel, there's no one here but us."

He closed his eyes and shook his head.

Jacinda drew closer, wrapping them both in the comforter, her naked warmth seeping into his bones.

"Just a nightmare," she said softly. "It's okay."

But it was so much more than that.

Gabriel was almost afraid to look at her again, so certain he'd see the succubus, or discover that he'd fallen into another fucked-up dream loop. But when he finally found the courage to open his eyes, there was only Jacinda. Only the bright blue gaze of the witch he loved, searching his face, searching for the words to make everything better.

He cradled her face between his hands, his vision blurring with tears. "Bloody hell, Jacinda. Tell me it's you. Tell me you're real. Tell me I haven't lost my damn mind."

She smiled and rested her cheek against his chest, holding him close. "No promises on that last one, but it's definitely me, and I'm definitely real. Now tell me, Prince. What's got you so haunted?"

His answer was as honest as it could be.

"Demons and ghosts, little moonflower. Demons and ghosts."

CHAPTER TWENTY-SEVEN

Sitting on the couch in nothing but a pair of sweats, Gabriel stared into the flames he'd stoked back to life, trying to parse through the gruesome visions. Jacinda was in the kitchen, brewing up a drink he hoped would soothe his restless mind.

Despite the warmth of the fire and the sound of his woman humming away in the kitchen, Gabriel couldn't shake free of his ghosts.

The child had returned—if she'd ever left at all—and now stood beside the fire place, bright blood soaking her dress, hands held mischievously behind her back.

Every time he closed his eyes, he saw the movie of his nightmares, Jacinda's torture and death playing out in vulgar, agonizing detail.

Every time he opened them, he saw the child. Silently watching. Accusing. Warning. Of what, he could only imagine. So many things threatened his life now, the lives of his brothers, of Jacinda. The succubus was close, clawing at some invisible barrier around his mind, desperate to find a way back in.

And what if she did? Would he even know it? Would anyone know it? Or would he be made to slaughter the ones he loved, never questioning it?

"Here," Jacinda said, fracturing his dark thoughts. "Drink this."

He took the offered mug. "One of your strongest potions, I hope."

"Ha! Irish coffee, actually. I had to make do with what I found in the kitchen. But I did add a bit of cinnamon to the mix—always good for a magical boost."

Gabriel took a sip of the piping hot beverage. It was too sweet, too thick. Through a scowl, he said, "Congratulations. You've officially convinced me you're not a dream."

"You sure about that, Prince?" She took a seat on the couch next to him, stretching her bare legs over his thighs and bringing her own mug to her lips.

She wore nothing but his hoodie, and Gabriel couldn't resist running his hand along her smooth calves, her thighs. Right now, her presence—the silky feel of her skin, the steady beat of her heart, the scent of her—was the only thing that made any damn sense.

"The witch of my dreams would *never* try to pass off Bailey's and Folger's decaf as real Irish coffee," he said.

"Hey!" She smacked his shoulder. "Dream witch or not, a *good* witch always knows how to improvise."

He grumbled, then took another sip, more grateful for the heat than the flavor.

They sat for several long moments in silence, the fire popping, the muted tick of an old-fashioned clock in the kitchen counting off the time. The wind had died down outside, and now the snow fell soft and heavy, blanketing the grounds in a diamond-white sea.

If not for those damn demons and ghosts, it would've been a picture-perfect night.

"I saw the succubus, Jace," he finally admitted, still unwilling to say her name. "It wasn't a dream—not exactly." He told her about the visions at the bar, the ocean, hell. "I felt her trying to get inside my head. Like she wanted to pin me down, but couldn't. Not like before. All she could do was feed me bits and pieces of my worst fears."

"For whatever reason, you're able to resist her in ways no man ever could. That, coupled with the protection ritual…" Jacinda snuggled closer. "It makes sense that she can't completely infiltrate your mind."

"But she's trying."

Jacinda sighed. "She never stopped. She never *will* stop —not until she gets what she's after."

"Have you had visions?"

"No. That's the crazy thing. She wanted me to help her with the hell gates, but I haven't heard a peep since that night at Obsidian. It's way more terrifying that way."

"Seems like her M.O." He took another sip of the too-sweet coffee. The fire crackled. The child looked on.

The harder Gabriel tried to wish her away, the more firmly she seemed to embed herself.

Gabriel closed his eyes and let out a long, slow breath. He had to tell Jacinda about the girl. The change in her routine—the fresh blood, the warning about the wolf at the door—it was all too ominous to ignore, especially since it'd coincided with the succubus' attempted mental attack.

"There's... more," he finally said, meeting her gaze. "Not just your sister. Something from my past. I've never spoken of it—not to my brothers, not to anyone. It's... it's never left me. I fear it never will."

Jacinda's eyes widened, her body stiffening, as if she could feel the dark shift of his thoughts. The fear running beneath his words.

"Gabriel, what's wrong?"

The child stared at him. Flickered, then solidified once more.

Blood spilled like tears from her eyes.

Gabriel closed his hand around Jacinda's knee, anchoring himself, willing his heartbeat to steady, willing the vicious burn of guilt to subside.

"I need to tell you," he whispered, "about the time I killed the witch."

CHAPTER TWENTY-EIGHT

"After my family and I were turned into vampires," Gabriel said, "we were forced to live at the estate of House Kendrick—the old royal family. It was part of the deal my father made with the vampire king, long before he slaughtered him and usurped the throne: ten years of servitude to earn our immortal freedom."

Jacinda nodded. Gabriel suspected she'd picked up bits and pieces of their history from her time with Duchanes, perhaps from Chernikov or the other demons Duchanes liked to surround himself with. The rise and fall of Augustus Redthorne had always been a juicy topic among the supernatural elite.

"In a cottage in the woods bordering the estate, there lived an old witch," Gabriel continued, "just like in the stories my mother had read to me when I was a child."

"This witch... Was she dark? Light?"

"She was... determined. Clever. Utterly without

morals, good or bad, though it took me far too long to see it." He took another sip of the coffee. "Anyway, she found me wandering the woods one day, then the next, and another still. She was kind to me, and a good listener. Before I knew it, I was visiting her nearly every day, just for the company. Just to escape the cruelties of House Kendrick for a bit.

"She knew I hated being a vampire, and I knew she hated being alone, cast aside by her coven because she wasn't powerful enough. So one day, after a lengthy exchange of miseries, we struck a bargain: she'd find a way to cure my vampirism and return me to the humanity I so desperately missed, and in exchange, I would grant her the rights to... well, all of it, I suppose."

"All of what?"

"Me." Gabriel turned back toward the fire. The blood on the child's face had dried into two black rivers that sliced down her cheeks. "From that moment forward, the kind witch I'd known and even liked was gone."

He closed his eyes, the remembered pain arcing through his body as if it'd happened only yesterday.

"Every night I would go to her, as agreed, lying on a stone altar in the woods in mute horror as she carved into my flesh, drained my blood until I was nearly desiccated, injected me with one potion after another, forced me to..." He shifted on the couch, shame pooling in his gut. "I suppose she wasn't unlike a succubus in some ways, though it wasn't pleasure or pregnancy she sought. She said it was all for her magic—that she needed to practice, to gain strength and skill in order to perform the ritual to cure me, or it would never work."

When Gabriel met Jacinda's gaze, he saw the fury in her eyes, the same that'd burned through him all those nights, all those months the witch had defiled him in the woods.

"Eventually," he continued, "she admitted that she couldn't help me. That her magic wasn't strong enough to counter vampirism, that I needed to accept my fate and embrace immortality. It was at the end of a particularly torturous night of experimentation, and in that moment, lying on her work table beneath the trees, watching her pour a bottle of my blood onto the ground, I'd never felt so helpless and broken. Not when I found my father out in the barn with Nuisance. Not even on the night I was turned into a vampire against my will, forced to watch my mother and youngest siblings die."

A log shifted on the fire, unleashing a cascade of sparks and pops that made him flinch.

"She looked at me with pity, Jacinda. Like I should've known better. And in that instant, I remembered my father's words about mercy and vowed I would never let her—or anyone else—make me feel helpless again.

"I feigned weakness, waiting for her to draw close to collect her tools. As soon as she was within my grasp, I tore the heart from her chest, sank my fangs into her neck, and drained every last drop of blood from her body. Repayment for the blood she'd stolen from me." He turned to look at Jacinda once more, a tear slipping down his cheek. "I murdered her, Jacinda, because she betrayed me. Lied to me. Tortured me for months and I just… I couldn't let it stand."

"The witch's death was a far kinder end than she deserved," Jacinda said, sitting up so she could touch his face, soft and gentle and heartbreaking. That such a beautiful thing could exist in the same realm as this brutal story was a paradox he couldn't comprehend.

"There's more." He turned away again, unable to accept the kindness of her touch. "There was a… child. A little girl. Four, maybe five years of age. The witch's daughter. I hadn't known she was there. Hadn't known she'd even *existed* until the moment I tossed her mother's limp body to the ground, and she darted out from behind the trees."

Jacinda gasped, and Gabriel simply nodded, continuing his abhorrent confession. "There was no questioning her identity. She was the spitting image of the witch. She glanced down at the body, then at me, the silence deafening. For a moment she just watched me, frozen, a tiny furrow appearing between her eyebrows. I didn't know what to say to her. What to do. I was equally frozen. Equally lost.

"Finally, she knelt by the body and reached for the woman's hand. Tried to shake her awake, urgently, desperately, and I…" Every word sliced through his throat like a razor blade, making it harder to breathe. To speak. "It was a long time before she stopped. She looked up at me once more, and she just… The child knew her mother was dead. It was in her eyes—that acceptance. A realization that the woman had fallen by my hand. By my fangs."

Now, the ghost-child approached him, so close he could've touched her if he'd dared. She stood at his feet, her eyes sinking into deep pits inside her skull, as black as the dried blood on her porcelain-pale cheeks.

"I dropped to my knees and took her hands," he said, more to the child than to Jacinda. "I told her my name. I told her my father's name. What we were. I told her that when she came of age and came into her power, if she still remembered me, she was welcome to hunt me down and take her revenge in whatever way she saw fit. I promised I wouldn't fight her. That I'd submit to her willingly."

"Did she come for you?" Jacinda asked, her voice a ragged whisper, her eyes boring deep as if she, too, could see through his soul, right down to the guilt that still burned as hot as an ember inside. "Did she get her revenge?"

A broken smile touched his lips as the child's face continued to blacken before his eyes. "She never left me, Jacinda. Perhaps *that's* her revenge."

He told her about the ghost-girl, about how she'd watched him at different times throughout his life. How she'd come to him again tonight, this time covered in fresh blood, warning about the wolf at the door.

Gabriel didn't even know if the child had ever come of age in life. In his visions, she was always young. Always dressed as she had been on that day, just as he'd left her, too cowardly to do anything else.

Perhaps she'd died that day too, just like her mother.

He'd abandoned her. A child, alone in the woods. It was

a sin more grievous than the murder that'd made her an orphan. A sin more grievous than all the monsters he'd slaughtered, all the souls he'd sent to hell.

"You did what you had to do to survive," Jacinda said.

His broken smile turned into a bitter laugh. "That's what we have to tell ourselves in order to survive the things we supposedly had to do to survive."

"Gabriel," she said softly, reaching for him, but he didn't deserve forgiveness or redemption, least of all from Jacinda.

He didn't deserve *her*.

He told her as much, pushing away her tender touches.

Ignoring his refusal, Jacinda removed the mug from his hands, set it on the end table with hers. Climbed into his lap and straddled him. Took his face between her hands.

"Gabriel." Her tone was firm and commanding now, and he finally looked up at her, those blue eyes flickering in the firelight, full of passion. Full of fire. "You've made your confessions tonight. Now I need to make mine."

Her hair spilled down over her shoulders, tickling his chest.

"Somewhere between the night I threatened to grind your bones into dust and the night you put me to work behind the bar... Somewhere between you ditching me in the wine cellar after getting me all hot and bothered and me ditching you in a ritual bath... Somewhere between begging you for that first kiss in your bedroom and another one tonight in the Gardens... Somewhere between dropping that first bottle of Bordeaux and sharing the second tonight under the most beautiful stars in the galaxy… I fell in love with you too, Gabriel Redthorne. Madly, terrifyingly, obsessively in love with you. So I don't care what you think you deserve or don't deserve, because I'm already yours. I've *always* been yours, and no ghosts from the past can change that. Now kiss me, before I have to bust out the hellfire."

It flashed in her eyes, a warning and a promise.

And before him, the child flickered and vanished.

Gabriel slid his hands inside the back of Jacinda's sweatshirt, pulling her close.

"You mean *everything* to me," he whispered against her mouth. "Absolutely everything, and devil help the monster who tries to take you from me."

Then he claimed her mouth, tasting a hint of her smoky hellfire, breathing her in, devouring her, sealing the promises they'd both made tonight with a searing kiss that burned hotter than fire.

But when he finally pulled back to look at her face, to take a breath, to tell her again how much he loved her, the ghost-girl emerged from the darkness once more.

She no longer held her hands behind her back, but out in front of her chest.

And there, clutched in her tiny fists, spilling blood down both her arms, was the severed head of a wolf.

A cruel smile twisted her face, revealing black teeth in a black mouth.

"I told you, vampire prince," she hissed. "There's a wolf at the door."

She turned abruptly and headed for the exit, vanishing the moment she reached the door.

Gabriel slid out from beneath Jacinda and followed the girl's path, shoving his feet into his boots and wrenching open the door.

Outside, the world was silent and white, save for the cherry-red stain spreading across the snow at the bottom of the steps.

"Gabriel, what's wrong?" Jacinda crowded behind him, peering out from over his shoulder. "Holy fuck!"

A wolf lay in a pool of blood, its head severed from its body, a light dusting of snow covering its fur. Steam rose up where the blood met the ice.

A fresh kill.

"Cole!" Jacinda cried, trying to push past him.

He wrapped her in his arms and hauled her against his chest. "No. It's not a shifter. Just a regular wolf. A warning."

"But who the fuck would—"

A ringing in the cabin, a harsh buzz clattering against the table.

Gabriel's cell.

They dashed back inside, adrenaline flooding them both. With a trembling hand, Gabriel picked up the phone. Glanced at the number flashing across the screen.

No name, just a city: Newark, New Jersey.

He answered on speaker, heart ready to pound out of his chest. "Who the fuck is this?"

"Gabriel Redthorne," came the smug, oily reply. "My old friend. I trust you got my delivery?"

Jacinda turned as white as the snow.

"Duchanes," Gabriel ground out. "What the fuck do you want? Where did you get this number?"

"You know, I've been running some experiments—wait, what am I saying? Of *course* you know that. You know everything about me, thanks to your spy dogs."

A bolt of fear arced through Gabriel's chest. "What the bloody hell did you do?"

"I've made a fascinating discovery is all," he said, clearly amused at the distress he was causing. "Quite a thing to witness."

"Out with it," Gabriel demanded.

"Wolves and silver," he said. "Liquified, injected directly into the veins. Honestly, I never expected such a fervent response."

Underscoring the point, a wolf howled in the background, pained. Tortured. A howl that could only belong to Cole.

The sound of it set Gabriel's teeth on edge.

"Trust me when I tell you," Gabriel growled, his voice a deadly warning, "you *don't* want to do this, Duchanes."

"You know, if I had a dollar for every time a Redthorne vampire has informed me of what I do and do not want to do—"

"You'd be able to afford a luxurious tomb instead of the nameless dirt hole I'm going to dump your ashes in. State your fucking terms, Duchanes. Now."

"I'm so glad you brought that up," Duchanes said.

Gabriel met Jacinda's gaze, her eyes alight with hellfire, their hearts pounding out the same wild beat.

He reached for her hand. Squeezed it tight.

Whatever came next, they were in it together. Partners. Always. Forever.

"One term," Duchanes said, and the wolf howled again, then whimpered. "Nonnegotiable. I'm tired of playing games with—"

"Say it!" Gabriel roared, though he already knew the answer. Knew it from the moment he saw the Jersey number flash on his screen.

Knew it from the moment he charged into Bloodbath two months ago, slaughtered most of House Duchanes, and claimed Jacinda for his own.

"I want my witch returned to me," the vampire bastard finally said. "Or the next dead wolf you find on your doorstep will be the one you once called a friend."

It's not over yet! Gabriel and Jaci's story continues in Heart of Flames!

The vampire prince and his little moonflower have finally admitted their feelings for each other, but the real battles are just beginning. Deadly enemies, a blood curse with no easy cure, and the darkest powers of hell are all converging, ready to destroy everything—and *everyone*—they hold dear...

Find out what happens next in **Heart of Flames, book three of the Vampire Royals of New York: Gabriel series!**

Have you read Dorian and Charlotte's epic love story yet?

Catch up on the original VRNY series, starting with book one, **Dark Deception!** Read on for a sexy little sneak peek…

Vampire lovers! If you loved reading this story as much as I loved writing it, come hang out with me and the other amazing Vampire Royals of New York fans in our private Facebook group, Sarah Piper's Sassy Witches. Pop in for sneak peeks, cover reveals, exclusive giveaways, book chats, and plenty of complete randomness! We'd love to see you there.

XOXO
Sarah

"I'll keep *all* your secrets, love." Dorian covered the woman's delicate fingers, holding her hand firmly against his chest. "Though I strongly caution you against deceiving me."

She gazed up at him through dark, feathery lashes and bit her lower lip, likely buying more time to invent her excuse. The woman was no louse in the fine art of seduction, and she was clearly up to no good. But what *kind* of no good, Dorian could only speculate. Robbery was top of his mind, but if that were the case, she had very few options for hiding her treasure; that hot little dress was definitely *not* made for smuggling.

"I have reason to believe the family is on the verge of bankruptcy," she finally said. "I heard they might consider offers for pieces not officially on the block."

Dorian laughed. "Considering what I paid for that painting, it's likely they're back in the black."

"Three million dollars? Doubtful. That's a drop in the bucket for these people."

"*These* people?" He raised an eyebrow, gaze sweeping up from her designer shoes to the tasteful but nevertheless authentic diamonds studding her earlobes. The woman even *smelled* rich—a combination of scents so firmly embedded in his mind it would follow him through eternity.

Who did she think she was fooling?

"I just meant…" She closed her mouth and pulled away from his grasp, doing her best to mask her irritation. When she spoke again, her voice had softened considerably. "It's a terrible situation. They have a lot of debt. The penthouse is in foreclosure. They're actually moving overseas."

Trading gossip about other people's misfortunes was beneath him, but he suspected her theory was true. He'd been gouged on the painting, but they would've settled for a lot less if she and Duchanes hadn't run up the bidding.

"I fail to see what their financial situation has to do with your sneaking around."

"It has everything to do with it," she snapped, her cheeks blushing with frustration and more than a little arousal. "But nothing to do with *you*. So if you don't mind, please show yourself out."

"You expect me to turn my back on a potential crime in progress?"

"I expect you to… Look, I totally appreciate the earlier save. Who knows what that creep would've done if you hadn't ridden in on your white horse? And thanks for the drinks, and the fun conversation, and..." She closed her eyes and blew out a breath, shaking her head as if she were having an argument with her own mind.

Dorian wasn't sure who won, but when she looked at him again, her eyes blazed with fresh anger.

"But seriously," she said. "It doesn't concern you."

"I see." Dorian offered a wry smile. Trouble or not, her feistiness turned him on beyond reason. The attitude, the taser, the spark of disobedience in her eyes...

You need to be tied up and spanked, little prowler.

Blood and power hummed through his veins, the image of his handprint on her bare flesh igniting a different sort of hunger inside.

This long into an immortal life, there were few things Dorian still enjoyed. The company of a beautiful woman was, on occasion, one of them.

But nothing—*nothing*—made him harder than a woman with fire. A woman who could hold her own, even as she begged to be dominated.

Soon enough, he'd have her doing both.

He took a step toward her, the soft thud of her pulse an erotic drumbeat that damn near hypnotized him.

For a moment, her anger faded, and she held his gaze in silence, tension crackling between them, her breath shallow, mouth slightly parted. She bit her bottom lip again, and he stared eagerly, already imagining the sweet taste of her kiss, the dangerous tease of her blood as his fangs grazed the plump flesh...

"The painting," she said suddenly, breaking the trance.

She turned toward the fireplace, gesturing at the art displayed over the mantle. "Heinrich von Hausen's *Adrift*. One of his lesser known works, but still a masterpiece by any measure."

"You'll have to try harder than that," he said. "You've already impressed me with your knowledge of art."

"I'm not trying to impress you. I'm trying to tell you that *this* painting is one of my favorites. My father took me to see it at the Smithsonian when I was a kid. How it ended up here, I can only imagine. But as soon as I saw it, I knew I wanted to ask the owners about it. Maybe arrange for a private bid, or… I don't know. Something."

An echo of sadness lingered in her voice, as raw and authentic as the painting itself, chased by a wave of the same darkness he'd seen earlier, rising anew in her eyes.

If he'd met her a hundred years ago—fifty, even— maybe he would've asked her about it. Offered comfort. Promises. Hell, maybe he'd have marched right back into the auction room, tracked down the host, and bought the damn painting for her on the spot, just to make her smile.

But these days, there was no room in his heart for sentimentality.

Only hunger.

Only desire.

In a flash, he closed the last of the distance between them, forcing her to take a step back, then another. Her shoulders hit the door of a small closet, and she dropped her purse and gasped, looking up at him with a mix of fear and lust, a combination that all but sealed her fate.

"Touching story." He trailed a finger across her exposed collarbone. Not far below, the curve of her breasts peaked out over the top of her dress, full and inviting. It was another of her many contradictions—hot and hard on the inside, soft and elegant on the outside—and Dorian couldn't wait to make her unravel. To expose every last one of her secrets—mind, body, and soul. "Forgive me if I don't quite buy it."

"What… what are you doing?" she whispered, heart fluttering like a hummingbird, the swell of her breasts rising and falling with every frightened breath.

But the scent of her desire didn't lie.

Dorian reached up and cupped her face, dragging his thumb across those plump lips, already imagining what they'd feel like wrapped around his cock. What she'd look like on her knees, wrists bound behind her back, *begging* him for it.

But when it came to pleasure, he was a master of… Well, some might call it patience. He preferred a more accurate descriptor.

Restraint.

It was an exquisite torture, the administration of which brought him as much pleasure as the ultimate surrender.

As badly as he wanted to fuck her hot mouth, to unleash every bit of pent-up yearning her presence had stirred to life inside him, he was even more desperate to taste her. To drive her to the knife's edge between pleasure and pain, and watch her fall over the precipice, her body submitting to his every command.

He lowered his hand again, fingers skimming the top edge of her dress, the heat of her skin weakening his resolve.

A soft moan escaped her lips, despite her best efforts to contain it. Her eyelids fluttered closed.

"Ah, there's nothing quite like a bad girl in a beautiful dress," he murmured, and she arched her back, bringing her breast to his palm. Beneath his touch, her taut nipple rose against the fabric. "I suppose you think that's enough to make me fall at your feet, lapping up your lies like a starved kitten at the milk bowl."

"I didn't… I was trying to… I'm…" She tripped over her words, her breathing turning more erratic with every gentle stroke. "It's not a lie. I—"

"Shh." Dorian ran his hand down to her rib cage, thumb teasing her nipple, his other hand sliding into the hair gathered at the base of her neck. The silky knot came loose from its binds, long auburn locks tumbling over her shoulders and unleashing more of the citrus-and-vanilla scent that made his head spin.

"If I were a decent man," he said, "I'd haul you out to security and pat myself on the back for saving the poor bastard who owns this place from whatever schemes you're undoubtedly planning."

Dorian released her neck, and she opened her eyes, irises nearly swallowed by the dark pupils.

He pressed a finger to her lips to silence another excuse. The soft heat of her breath ghosted across his fingertip, the promise of her wet mouth making his cock throb.

"But since I'm *not* a decent man," he said, "I'm going to make you an offer instead. Two choices. Think very, very carefully about your response—I'm only going to ask once. Understand?"

She nodded, blood pulsing visibly beneath the pale skin of her throat, every heartbeat a seductive whisper, a promise, a warning.

Don't do this, Redthorne. You know what happens…

Ignoring the voice of reason, he gazed into her beautiful, devious eyes, his cock so hard it fucking *ached*.

"Option one," he said. "You walk out that door right now, take the elevator to the ground floor, and disappear. Don't return to this building. Don't return to this neighborhood. Forget we ever crossed paths."

"What's… what's option two?"

"Option two." Dorian lowered his mouth to hers, so close he could taste the gin on her tongue, and fisted her dress, hiking it up to reveal her bare, toned thighs. He slid a hand between them, wet heat radiating through the thin black lace of her panties. With the softest brush of his lips against hers, he whispered, "I'm tearing off this *pathetic* scrap of lace, dropping to my knees, and fucking you with my mouth until I'm absolutely *convinced* you'll never look at another painting again without recalling the time a stranger cornered you in the study at the Salvatore penthouse and forced you to come for him, again… and again… and again."

She drew a sharp breath, and he increased the pressure between her thighs, dragging his knuckles back and forth.

"So what's it going to be, little prowler? Will you go, or will you…" He arched his hand up, pushing hard against the damp fabric. "…come?"

"*Fuck.*" The whisper fell against his lips, her hips rocking as Dorian restarted the slow, teasing strokes.

"What's that, gorgeous? I didn't quite catch your answer."

"Fuck off," she said, feisty until the very end. Then, with new heat blazing in her eyes, "God, I want option two. Fucking give me option two."

"Good answer, love. Because here's *my* secret." He hooked his fingers into the panties, and with a swift jerk of his wrist, tore them from her body like tissue paper. "You never really had a choice."

Ready for more of vampire king Dorian and the seductive little thief out to steal more than just his heart? Grab your copy of **Dark Deception!**

ABOUT SARAH PIPER

Sarah Piper is a Kindle All-Star winning urban fantasy and paranormal romance author. Through her signature brew of dark magic, heart-pounding suspense, and steamy romance, Sarah promises a sexy, supernatural escape into a world where the magic is real, the monsters are sinfully hot, and the witches always get their magically-ever-afters.

Her recent works include the newly released Vampire Royals of New York series, the Tarot Academy series, and The Witch's Rebels, a fan-favorite reverse harem urban fantasy series readers have dubbed "super sexy," "imaginative and original," "off-the-walls good," and "delightfully wicked in the best ways," a quote Sarah hopes will appear on her tombstone.

Originally from New York, Sarah now makes her home in northern Colorado with her husband (though that changes frequently) (the location, not the husband), where she spends her days sleeping like a vampire and her nights writing books, casting spells, gazing at the moon, playing with her ever-expanding collection of Tarot cards, binge-watching Supernatural (Team Dean!), and obsessing over the best way to brew a cup of tea.

You can find her online at SarahPiperBooks.com and in her Facebook readers group, Sarah Piper's Sassy Witches! If you're sassy, or if you need a little *more* sass in your life, or if you need more Dean Winchester gifs in your life (who doesn't?), come hang out!

Printed in Great Britain
by Amazon